Dancing on Broken Ankles

Book One: Dancing on Broken Ankles Series

J.P. Sterling

Contents

This book is dedicated to the ballerina in my life.
Never stop dancing. I love you for always – no matter what.

Chapter One

St. Augustine wrote: "Learn to dance, so when you get to heaven the angels know what to do with you." I always thought that was a pleasant image for people who like to think about the pleasantries of the afterlife. But for me, I knew I first needed to get through this life. So, for now—I dance to forget.

With my dance bag balanced on my shoulder, I eased through the front door of my house and softly latched the lock behind me. Lingering in the entryway, I could hear my dad's baritone voice boom from the kitchen. "What do you think I'm doing?"

"I don't know anymore. That's why I asked." My mom's reply was just another forlorn attempt to make my dad empathize with her, but I knew neither my dad nor I had much empathy left for her.

"I don't get why you don't trust me." He sounded exhausted.

"Because you didn't tell me the truth right away. I had to find out from your mother, of all people!"

I shut my eyes, hoping to become invisible. Last week, I had found my mom crying alone in her darkened bedroom after my dad had stormed out of the house. I had also noticed she stopped wearing makeup. This is what she did when she had crying spells. It was easier to not put on makeup than to try to clean a smeared-up mess. Hearing them argue again, I tiptoed toward the kitchen, listening unashamedly.

"You never forget anything, do you? I wish I could be perfect like you," my dad replied. I absorbed his words with my eyes still closed. I hated the feeling I got when I heard them fight. I held my breath, trying to go unnoticed in the deafening silence.

In a defeated voice, my mom finally broke the air. "This isn't working anymore, Cole. So much has changed."

"I agree. I wish I could do so many things differently, but life doesn't give you any do-overs. I can't live my life with this hanging over my head every day. We need to move past it." My dad's voice was sorrowful, making me wonder what he had done.

"Wanda said she can have the house on the market by Monday if we sign the papers today." I cringed. *They're selling the house. That's messed up. Where are we going to live?*

"Did she say what we can get for it?" Dad asked.

"She said the Becker's house down the street sold for one-point-two mil. She thought the market has gone up a little since then."

"That's not too bad. It would give us more than enough money to start over."

"A fresh start is exactly what we all need."

I was dumbfounded and had no idea why we would move. My mind raced through all the signs that I had been witnessing over the last month: arguing, conversations about money, weird fights about responsibilities. They even quizzed me last week about the worth of my private school education.

I didn't want to move, but the more I thought about it, I knew I'd be okay if I had to leave my house. My friend, Tina, moved a few years ago after her mom died. She got a dog to keep at her new house, but I doubt my mom would let me have a dog. She doesn't like animals. In fact, she doesn't like most things. She walks around with a fuzzy unibrow all the time because she's forever upset her life isn't what she had planned.

Their argument had fizzled to a silence, so I opened the hall closet and purposely let my dance bag drop noisily to the floor to announce my arrival.

"Abs?" Mom called.

"Yeah."

"I'm making dinner. You hungry?" Dad said.

"Can I eat in my room?" I walked into the kitchen, finding a pan of my dad's famous enchiladas cooling on the top of the stove.

"You not feeling well?" Dad raised an eyebrow toward me.

"I'm okay. I want to start studying for my math exam tomorrow." It was partly true. I left out the part about how I couldn't stand any longer because my ankle was killing me. My dancing was one of the issues that gave my mom a fuzzy unibrow. She would use any excuse she could come up with for me to not participate, and she'd pounce on it like a cat locked in a cage with a bird. Without waiting for permission, I dished up an enchilada, grabbed a napkin and fork, and headed toward my room.

"Don't forget we have dinner tomorrow night with the Rogers," my dad called after me.

"I didn't forget." I moaned. The Rogers were my parents' best friends. They had two kids. Their daughter, Milly, was super sweet and in the second grade. She loved unicorns and dolls. She was fun to have around, but then there was her brother, Fulton, who was a year older than me. We'd been forced together our whole lives. It wasn't bad when we were little because we'd swim or ride bikes, but the older we got, the stranger he became. Most of the time he would watch me and not talk. He towered over me in height, and he had a habit of standing way too close. I didn't know if he was shy or what, but he breathed so heavily it was all I could hear when he was in the room. It creeped me out.

"Abs," my dad's softer voice called after me.

"Yeah." I slowed my steps.

"Dr. Webber's office called today to confirm your appointment tomorrow. Mom has meetings all afternoon, but I freed up an hour. Do you want me to pick you up from school?"

"Whatever," I said. "But don't come inside. Text me and I'll meet you in the parking lot." My parents were so embarrassing that I didn't want to risk them doing something in front of my friends.

I went into my room without waiting to hear him reply, but not before I heard my mom say, "She's such a snot."

Dad replied, "You raised her."

***

"Are you going to eat your lunch?" Tina eyed my salad plate the following day at school.

"Nah, I have to get weighed at the doctor." I pushed my cut-up pieces of chicken around my plate. It was a trick I learned to do when I wasn't going to eat but didn't want people to know I was wasting food.

"What do you have to worry about? You're a beanpole," Becky quipped.

"I don't like getting weighed."

"So, what's your doctor's appointment about this time? Your knee again?" Becky asked between bites of her sandwich.

"My ankle." I reached for my bottle of water and started to pick at the label. I hated talking about this stuff.

"Man, you're falling apart," Tina said. "Weren't you just having issues with your hip, too?"

"The life of a ballerina must be rough." Becky sounded generally concerned.

"Well, not normally this bad," I said. "I have some weird issue with my tendons that make them overly bendy and stretchy. I was born like that. See, look how I can pull my fingers." I pulled my thumb all the way back until it touched the back of my hand.

"Gross. Don't show me that when I'm eating." Tina jerked her head away, shifting a thick lock of her sunshine-colored hair to fall in front of her shoulder.

"I think it's cool." Becky leaned closer to look at my thumb. "Do all your fingers do that?"

"Everything does. My legs. My arms. It's why I'm so flexible. But it comes with a price. My tendons continue to stretch, and as they do, they get thinner, and I lose stability."

"That's what Erica was talking about," Tina said.

I turned my head toward her. "What did you hear Erica say?"

"She said you were falling all over the place in dance. I think she's still secretly jealous you got to be the principal ballerina last year."

"What else did she say?" I asked, leaning in closer.

"Nothing really. She was laughing about how silly you looked."

"She needs to learn to keep her mouth shut or she'll regret it."

"Not to change the subject," Tina interjected, "but my dad has to go to the Middle East next week for some work thing."

"That sounds awful," Becky said.

"No, it's awesome because Bimbo is on the west coast for a modeling thing," Tina said. "I get to stay home alone. My dad's having the neighbor lady spy on me, but they didn't even think about the beach house. So, guess what?"

"You want to have a party at your dad's beach house?" Becky squealed.

"Get the word out. Tomorrow night. I want to make sure it gets all over school, so Benson hears."

"You still like him?" Becky asked.

Tina gave her an affirming smile.

"Can I ride with you?" Becky asked Tina.

"I thought you got your license?"

Becky rolled her eyes. "Don't ask."

"You failed?" Tina asked.

Becky's sea-colored eyes got wide. "No, I passed. But my parents are mad at me for my math grade, so they won't buy me a new car until I get it up to an A. They want me to drive my brother's old car. It's like a 2010 four-door. I told my mom my grade wasn't even that bad, and at least I didn't get a forty-one percent on my midterm like Abs."

I glared at her while the panic seeped into my throat. "You told your mom about my math midterm?"

"I had to. She thinks I'm the dumbest person in school because I have a B."

"So, you corrected her opinion by letting her know I'm actually the dumbest person?" I looked away. Becky was the smartest of my friends and usually the nicest, but sometimes her naivety made her do the stupidest stuff.

"I'm sorry, Abs, but I'd die if anyone saw me driving that car. Your parents bought you a new car and you have way worse grades."

"Just don't bring me into your conversations with your mom, please. Your mom tells my mom everything."

Tina laughed a high-pitched laugh. "You girls are so weird. I have a C in math, but that's because Mr. Schloz changed my grade for me."

"How he'd do that?" I kept my brow lowered in skepticism.

"He was showing us our grades in class one day by calling us over to his computer. I had a D. I didn't care. I hate math. I was about to go sit, and then he said, 'Suppose you got an eight out of ten on this quiz instead of a five.' Then he switched it. I didn't say anything, and he continued to add points to all my quizzes, and boom, I got a C."

"That's dishonest," I said, half jealous he didn't switch my grade.

"It's because you play volleyball. He has a thing for his volleyball girls," Becky said. "I heard he did the same thing to Kinsley."

"That's totally creepy. Someone should report him," I said.

"No, don't do that. Then I'll get my D back. Anyway, getting back to my party." Tina looked over at me. "What's up with you? Do you want to ride with us?"

"I can't. I have this dinner thing with my parents."

"What kind of dinner thing?" Tina asked.

"A thing with the Rogers. I heard my parents talking about selling our house, and I think they are planning to tell me then," I said matter-of-factly because I didn't care. I wasn't in the mood to go to Tina's party, and I wasn't happy about the dinner, but I hoped it would be enough of an excuse for them to drop it.

"Really? Why are they selling your house?" Becky said.

"I knew it." Tina waved her salad fork at me.

I looked up. "You did? How?"

"Your dad. I see him all over town with other women. He's always out at coffee shops or out for lunch. He's too good looking to spend that much time with all those women. My mom's always commenting about how he has coffee with a different woman every day. I bet your parents are separating."

I furrowed my eyebrows. "Nah, my parents wouldn't separate. And I don't think it's my dad's issue. It's more my mom's. My dad's out a lot because that's how he does business. He says his job is to *woo them and wow them*—as far as his clients go, that is. He woos them into his office, and then once he gets the job, he wows them with his presentations."

Tina gave me a horrified look. "Your dad says his job is to woo them and wow them, and you don't see that being problematic to your parents' marriage?"

I shook my head. "No. That's just him. He's always thinking in little riddles, or elevator pitches, as he calls them. He has a slogan for everything. He's a creative type. It has nothing to do with meeting other women. He calls it branding."

I could tell both Tina and Becky were unconvinced, but they were content to let silence loom. My phone beeped. It was my dad. "I have to go," I said. "Time to go get weighed."

Chapter Two

"Aubergine White." Dr. Weber held his hand out for me.

"Abs." I felt the dry skin from his palm scratch my hand when I shook it.

"Just Abs?" He looked at me curiously.

"Yep."

"You have the most colorful name I've seen. One of your parents must be an artist." He sat on his rolling stool, letting his belly roll over his belt when he leaned forward to look at the computer screen.

My dad spoke up. "I'm in marketing. I spend my days trying to make boring people look attractive. When we had a baby, I wanted a name that was unique and stood out."

Dr. Webber's lips curled into a full smile. "It is different."

I kept my head down because I hated when my dad referred to my name as another marketing gimmick. Deep down, that's what I felt about our lives. Perfect to everyone else, but in real life, our family was a mess.

When Dr. Webber finished reviewing my digital chart, he walked over to me. "I'm going to have you slide back and rest your foot on the bed." I scooted back and watched as he felt my foot and flexed it up and down. "You definitely have too much range of motion. I can see why you're having accidents." His eyes met mine. "I looked at your X-rays, and your tendons appear healthy enough for me to go in to clip and shorten. Then I'll reattach them and it will tighten everything up. We do an epidural for those surgeries, so you won't feel anything." He winked as if it confirmed everything would be well.

Lowering my eyes again, I waited for my dad to bring up the question I wouldn't dare to ask. "Abs is a talented ballerina. How will this affect that?"

Dr. Webber looked back at me. "It doesn't really make sense for me to do the surgery if you think you want to continue dancing."

"What?" My chin rose.

With his low voice, which I now understood to be his bad-news voice, Dr. Webber added, "It means you're too young to be having these issues. You stretched out your tendons, making them thinner. I can shorten them. However, they're still stretchier than they should be. If you continue to dance, they'll stretch out again, causing them to get even thinner. Dancing accelerates the process."

"What happens if I decide to continue to dance after the surgery?" I avoided looking at my dad because I knew he would give me a disapproving look.

"Your tendons can only get so thin, and then they will start to rip. I will then have to go and repair them, but eventually they will be too weak to even do that. This isn't your average athletic injury where, if I fix it, it'll heal and do what it should. This is your body not working. It's best you accept this now, because you need your body."

"Dancing's what I know," I defended.

"You're young. You have lots of time to find a new hobby. Maybe take up painting, since your name's already suited for it." He smiled genuinely. "I can already see your gorgeous signature on an oil painting canvas."

My dad gave me his "be strong" look. I knew he wouldn't tell me not to dance, but he would plead with me in his own way. "What happens if I decide to wait on the surgery?" I asked.

"If you want to try putting off the surgery for a while, you should be fine as long as you aren't stretching them in dance class. How well you do is in your hands. I've been doing this job long enough to know I can't convince people who don't want to be convinced."

I squared my shoulders. "I'm not going to stop dancing."

"Okay." He looked back at his computer screen and typed some notes into his computer. "I'm here if you decide to change your plans." He watched me like he expected me to change my mind immediately, but I pursed my lips together and avoided looking at my dad's pleading eyes.

That night, I rummaged through my bathroom cabinet to find my sports tape. I had a plan. If I kept my ankles wrapped tightly when I wasn't at dance, the tape would help to conserve them. I didn't think it was a big deal to be more flexible than I should be. I finished wrapping my ankles and went to sit at my desk in my room.

Feeling guilty, I looked online at some of the performers in the circus and how bendy they were. They could still walk. I decided

Dr. Weber didn't know what he was talking about. I closed my internet browser, but behind it another one had remained open, displaying my social media page. My eyes immediately landed on the "About Me" section, which said, "Aubergine White, Dancer."

I was a dancer. I couldn't remember starting dance, but my dad told me the story about how badly I wanted to be in the dance class. The class was for three-year-old kids who were potty trained, but even back then, I had a plan for everything. As soon as he had told me that, I potty trained myself, never to even have one single accident. So, I got to start class, and ever since then, I was a dancer. When I failed math, it didn't matter, because I could dance. When my friends were mean, I danced the pain away. When my mom was flashing her unibrow at me, I danced that away, too.

"Aubergine!" My mom's voice fog-horned through my bedroom door. I got off my bed and had every intention of going downstairs to have this duel out, but as soon as I turned my doorknob, the door flew backwards at me. My mom blew in like she was a tornado stirring around dust.

I backed against the wall. Her fuzzy unibrow was raging at me. Sometimes when she got like this, I would tune out the yelling, and I would daydream about taking my shaver and slicing out little pieces of her brow like I was playing Fruit Ninja.

"Are you going to tell me what you were up to today?"

"It sounds like you know."

"I got a text from Becky's mom. It looks like you girls are planning a party all the way out in Rockaway Beach tomorrow. Sue said she found messages on Becky's phone from over one hundred different kids, including boys who are sophomores in college! What are you guys thinking?"

My mind raced. She didn't know about my ankle. This argument wasn't even about me. It was about Becky. "I wasn't going to the party. I told them I had that dinner thing tomorrow."

She anchored both hands on her hips and her chin bobbled when she yelled, reminding me of a chicken clucking. "I'm not stupid. Your best friends are not going to plan a party and not invite you."

"They asked me, but I said I was busy."

"I can't believe you're able to look me in the face and tell me you had no plans of going. You're grounded."

Super glue. That's what I wanted to do with her unibrow. I could put a thin row of super glue on it and then smoosh it to the wall. Then when she backed away it would stay on the wall and I would be freed from it . . . but then I would have to look at it on my wall, which would be totally creepy. I turned my head down. "I know you don't believe me, and you aren't going to, but I wasn't planning on going."

"Not anymore, you're not. You can go to the dinner tomorrow, but you have to stay home the rest of the weekend." She started to leave the room, but then she turned on her heel and said, "And give me your credit card. No online shopping either."

I walked to my closet, pulled out my purse, took out my card, and walked it over to her. She took it. I imagined what it would be like if she would do something drastic like offer me a hug and tell me things would get easier at school, easier with friends, easier with my stupid ankles. But that's not my mom. Instead, she throbbed her unibrow at me. "Your life's about to change more than you could ever imagine." Her lips curled into a Cruella De-Vil smile. I half expected her to pull out a Dalmatian and start stroking it. She walked out and I slammed the door behind her.

Chapter Three

After school on Friday, I dominated in my dance class. I hit all my sequences perfectly, but I paid for it afterwards. I dragged my feet home to find three boxes in front of the house. They were all the results of my internet shopping bender I did a week earlier. I tore through the boxes to get rid of the evidence before my mom got home. She was sure to think this was something I did today, which would be against my shopping ban.

Two of the packages were shoe boxes: four-inch heels I vowed to no longer wear since I had to keep my ankles wrapped. The other box was a subscription box from my fashion stylist, providing me with a new outfit every month. I took all the boxes and tore them apart, dumping the evidence in the recycling bin. I then dashed through the house to stash my purchases in my bedroom before getting ready for our dinner.

We were meeting the Rogers at my parents' country club—which was great for me because they had a ton of salads on the menu and none of my friends ever went there so I knew no one would see me out in public with a bunch of weirdos. It was shocking how the Rogers kept getting weirder. When I was little, they would talk to my parents about normal stuff, like buying real estate and traveling, but as the years went on, they started talking less about real estate in terms of houses and more about the need to buy land.

I had no idea why they wanted a bunch of empty land. Eddie Rogers was my dad's best friend, and he was always talking about the need to have survival skills. I would usually just tune out the conversations and ask Millie if she needed me to braid her hair. She was usually compliant with my need to escape into something more normal.

Since the dreaded dinner was rapidly approaching, I needed to get dressed. After finding nothing to wear from my subscription box, I threw the rejected clothes onto my bed and headed toward my closet. I reached down and tugged behind a pile of clothes on the floor. I knew there were a couple of bags somewhere from when I had gone shopping a few weeks earlier. I found them underneath a new comforter set I had gotten a week ago but hadn't had the time to put on my bed yet.

One of the bags had a dress in it I loved, but I wasn't going to waste it on a dumb dinner like this. In the other bag, I had a pair of skinny jeans and a light-weight coral sweater. They were perfect because I could wear my riding boots with these pants, and I would have plenty of room for the pile of tape I would need to constrict my ankles.

My hair was still up in my required ballet bun. I doubled checked the back of it to make sure no shorter pieces of hair had fallen out. I brushed my hands over the top of my brunette hair to smooth out all the bumpy parts that had appeared from the bun loosening.

I stuck a couple bobby pins underneath the bun, pulling it tight again. I was ready to get this agony over with.

My parents were stupidly happy when we sat down and joined the Rogers. I looked around the table, and everyone except Fulton was cheerful. Fulton was staring at his menu like an alien spaceship had landed on the table and was now attempting to speak alien languages at him through a screen in his menu. Everyone said pleasant greetings, and then Millie blurted out something interesting: "I'm getting a pony!"

I waited for someone else to respond to her silliness, but when no one did, I took the bait. "That's great. Are you going to keep him in your townhouse?" I knew it was an attention-seeking game she had made up, because they lived in a thousand-square-foot condo in Midtown.

"No, when we move to the land, I'm getting my own pony. I'm going to name it Sundance."

I tried not to roll my eyes. Now Millie had joined the weird cult talk about moving to the land.

"Shhh," my mom said quietly to Millie, but her eyes were locked on me. I shot a curious look back at my mom, wondering why she was shushing a child.

My dad leaned over the table and directed a question toward Eddie. "I take it you told both your kids?"

"We told them last night. Millie's excited. Fulton's forlorn," Eddie said.

"Abs doesn't know yet," my dad said.

"What don't I know?" Nobody answered my question, so I asked another one. "What's Fulton forlorn about?" My eyes bounced from my dad to my mom to Fulton. Fulton didn't give me any clues and continued to stare straight into his alien spaceship menu. I knew my parents were referring to selling their house, but why would Fulton be forlorn about it?

"You don't know what we're celebrating tonight." My mom put on a deceptively warm smile. She then looked at my dad who lovingly grinned at her. "We were going to wait to tell you until everyone warmed up a little, but I don't see a reason to wait anymore, since Millie and Fulton know." She smiled at Millie, who wiggled in her chair like she was trying to hold in the secret by sitting on it. "We're celebrating today for many reasons. Number one, I put in my notice at the office. I'll be done working there in two weeks."

I let my mouth drop open. Now I was confused. Then my dad spoke, "I also put in my notice at work today."

I jolted so hard I should have gotten whiplash. My parents had lost their minds. I looked back to Fulton for a hint, but he was still lost in alien translation, and now I was jealous. Maybe those aliens knew what was going on. At the very least, it had to be a saner conversation than this one. The only words I could muster up were, "What's going on?"

I was searching for my mom's unibrow, but it wasn't there. I wanted to see it, to know it was her, but it was gone! This mom was not the mom I was used to. This mom had uplifted eyebrows, and I didn't like it. My uplifted-eyebrow mom said the words of doom I will never forget: "We're all moving to Montana to live off the land."

The aliens must have jumped out of Fulton's menu and infected my mom's brain, hijacking her words, because my mom never spoke like that. Eddie talks like that. "You're kidding, right?" I asked.

My mom beamed over at me and her lips moved with details, but they weren't all audible to me. I got dizzy. I heard words like solar-powered electricity, gardening, manual labor, fishing, gathering. Everyone was happy but Fulton. I listened as I heard more words about moving and selling the house, and my chest got tight. "Are you trying to kill me?" I said breathlessly as I held my chest.

With her mouth slightly agape, my mom looked at my dad, and then back at me. "No, Abs, but we do think we need a different way of life. We'll be able to get back to basics, spending real time with each other without all the distractions of city living."

I looked at Fulton. For the first time since we sat down, he returned my gaze, offering a weak smile like he felt my pain. "I can't move to Montana," I said. "I don't speak Spanish." I was grasping for anything to hold onto now. No one was coming to my defense.

"Montana, not Mexico," my dad said, sympathetically. "Montana's part of the United States. They speak English."

"Boy, your private school education must really be something," Eddie said, sealing his joke with a smile. It should have been friendly, but I found it insulting. Everyone burst out laughing. Everyone but Fulton, who for the second time looked at me with a sympathetic expression. I didn't want sympathy from Fulton Rogers, the biggest geek in school. This was a nightmare. I had to leave. I got up and bee-lined toward the door. My ankle faltered, and I leaned forward to stabilize myself. Apparently, there was a stupid, blind waiter carrying a tray of food who I didn't see. What I did see was the cascade of dishes crashing around me. In the distance, I heard my mom say, "Just let her go. She's going to have to adjust. She's used to being spoiled."

Chapter Four

I Ubered home, barricaded my bedroom door, flung myself onto my bed, and ugly cried for an hour. I had no idea what I was going to tell Tina and Becky. Sliding my laptop over in front of me, I opened my social media profile and stared at the "About Me" section: "Aubergine White, Dancer."

It all made sense to me now. The reason my parents didn't fight me to give up dance was because they knew it was going to come to an end anyway. Not only did I have to give up my identity as a dancer, but I had to quit my entire life! I used my mouse to highlight the word *dancer* behind my name. I was going to delete it like my parents were deleting my life. Then I imagined what I would put next to it now. *Farmer?* Gross. Never!

My dad knocked on my door. I knew it was my dad because my mom never knocked. "What?" My voice was nasally from crying.

"I brought your salad home since you didn't get a chance to eat it. Can I bring it in?"

"Sure."

He came in and placed the to-go box next to me. His eyes lingered on my computer screen, but he was respectfully quiet. It was too quiet, and I couldn't hold it in. I turned my face toward him. "Why, Dad? Is this about my ankles? I'll have the surgery."

"The surgery's totally up to you. I'm not going to fight you over something about your body, but we're going to Montana whether you have the surgery or not."

I sat up to plead with him. "Tell me this is all a joke to get me to behave better. I'll be better. I promise."

He reached forward and smoothed some hair that had fallen out of my bun. "It's not a joke, honey, but I understand why you're upset. It's a lot to take in."

"I'll get a math tutor so my grades will be better. I'll get nicer friends. I'll get a job. Whatever you want."

"It's not about that either."

"I'll cut up my credit cards. I'll never shop again. Take my cell phone or my car. I'll ride the bus everywhere. Please, Dad!" I pleaded so hard my stomach hurt.

"Someday you'll understand." His brown eyes softened with compassion.

"Never." I gritted my teeth as my despair changed to anger.

He reached over to my laptop and hit the delete button, making the word dancer disappear. His callousness toward my whole life's identity infuriated me. "Is this funny to you?" I squinted my eyes at him.

"Do you know why I named you Aubergine?"

Now I was annoyed. He was dodging the question and staying calm, which annoyed me even more. "You love eggplants?"

"Because Aubergine doesn't need a tagline."

I never understood why my dad always spoke in riddles, nor did I understand why he was doing this to me now. I must have been invisible, because he obviously couldn't see the agony I was enduring. "You deleted my identity."

His voice stayed low. "I know it feels like that to you now, but being a dancer is not your identity. It's a hobby, and one you're good at, but that's all—a hobby. I named you Aubergine because it's one of those names that doesn't need a tagline. All you need is Aubergine."

"That's dumb." I was mad and hurt, and I was getting madder. "How can you come in here and talk about this right now?" I screamed with hot tears welling in my eyes. "Can't you understand you just ruined my life!"

"Honey, our family got lost and we turned life into a big meaningless hustle. That's not what it should be. Your mom and I are simplifying things so we can focus on what really matters."

I closed my eyes, feeling defeated. "I can't talk to you anymore. Your metaphors are stupid. You're trying to spin this into a good thing. All I see is that you're quitting."

"I'm not quitting at all. Someday you will understand at a deeper level what this is for." He slowly backed toward the door. When I didn't acknowledge him anymore, he left my room, shutting the door behind him.

"You're gutting me," I whispered, but my words fell on no one.

After that, I only had two weeks until school was over before we had to move. Just two weeks to linger in my life as a dancer—as a city girl—and I relished every moment of it, finding a newfound gratitude for what I had lived. But then it was over, and just like that, the reset button was pressed on my life. I still felt that it was more like a delete than a reset, but nobody cared what I thought.

Chapter Five

Mom and I were the last to arrive in western Montana. My dad, who was already there, met us at the airport. He picked us up in a rusty, frog-green pickup. Mortified, I looked behind me to see who would witness me climb into this beast of a vehicle. I sighed out of relief that no one knew me here. At least I had that going for me.

I had been allowed to pack one suitcase, and out of principle I declined an actual suitcase and brought my dance bag instead. Out of everything I owned, my dance bag was probably my most prized possession. My dance teacher gave it to me after I had been awarded principal ballerina. She had my name embroidered on the side of it right next to our dance company logo. The bag wasn't worth any monetary value like most of my possessions I had to leave at home. However, it was one of those things that held the memories of my past as well as what all my future dreams *had* been.

My dad wrapped his arms all the way around my mom, giving her a longer than average hug. Even though I was avoiding looking at them, I could tell they were both emotional, and in a strange way that made me feel left out of their happiness club. We climbed into the single bench truck. My mom nestled into the middle and my dad placed his hand on her knee. I looked away, gluing my eyes to the window. This experiment of theirs was way out of hand. They could at least pretend to be empathic to what I was going through.

"What's with the frog truck?" I asked bitterly. My stomach was balled into a giant wad of knots. Some of them were nerves. Some of them were stress. Most of it was contempt for my parents.

"Like it?" My dad rested his elbow on the opened driver's side window. As he drove, the wind blew in, ruffling his dark hair that had grown out a little past his ears. It made him look unkept compared to his normally professional clean cut.

"Are you trying to kill me from embarrassment?" I was so disgusted with my parents that I sulked the entire drive. This move was completely irresponsible. They both quit lucrative careers, sold hard-to-find real estate, deserted friends, all to realize this little game they played with the Rogers of "let's move to the country." I was the only sane person. They were behaving like children. I needed this nightmare to be over.

"Abs . . ." Dad stole a look at me from behind the steering wheel, and I knew by the way he said my name that he was going into story mode, which meant it was my cue to tune him out. "The land we bought is five hundred acres in the Rocky Mountains. It's gorgeous and right on the edge of Glacier National Park. You can't find anything else like it."

"It truly is a dream location," my mom affirmed.

Dad continued: "There's only one road to our house, and I suspect with the amount of snow we're forecasted to get this winter that we might end up getting snowed in a time or two. We have some time to prepare, but we need to take this seriously or we will be in trouble."

"Snowed in?" I questioned. "How's that going to work when I have to go to school? You guys have been so secretive about everything. You haven't even told me anything about *where* I'll be going to school."

"That's the best part for you." He glanced at me briefly with a stupid smirk on his face. "You won't. We got you a home-study program. You can do everything you need to do right at the house. Of course, your real education will be learning from homesteading, but I knew you would want to have your traditional high school education too. The school we enrolled you in is fully accredited; you just need to upload assignments when you are done. It's so simple."

"I thought you said I won't have internet?"

"Yeah, we won't have internet at the cabin, but we'll make sure you're able to go to the library in town to do that. At least while the weather allows," he added.

"That's so generous of you," I said sarcastically. My heart twisted like it was choking underwater and struggling for fresh oxygen. I didn't even know I had been looking forward to going to school, but now it felt like my dad had ripped away the last little bit of my old life that I had been so desperately trying to hold on to. I wanted to argue, but I knew it was hopeless, and they didn't deserve to see me cry. I swallowed hard.

My dad steered the pickup into a clearing with three tiny buildings and a fenced pen where I could see a few baby animals. Inside the pen, Millie was bottle-feeding a lamb, and if I wasn't committed to being stubborn, I would have admitted the lamb was stinking cute.

Once the truck was parked, my dad hopped out and said, "Come, I'll show you to your room." With my bag on his shoulder, he waited for me to get out of the pickup.

"Where's the house?" I asked, surveying the land.

"Right there." He pointed to one of the buildings that was not much larger than a shed. "It's a tiny home. Completely off-grid with solar power upgrades."

I squinted my eyes to try to make the building look bigger, but it didn't work. I noticed it had what appeared to be a silly little porch on the front of it. If anyone else had told me they lived inside a house that small, I would have burst out laughing. I couldn't laugh now though, because it was me who was going to suffocate in that thing.

My dad took a deep breath and let it out. "I love the way the air smells here. Fresh evergreens."

Brain tumor. That had to be it. My dad wasn't well. He must have gotten some sort of brain tumor that caused him to think this was all a good idea. He needs a doctor, not a tiny home. I surveyed his body for signs of illness. I didn't see any irregularities. Maybe it wasn't cancer, but whatever it was must've been contagious, because all the previously sane adults—who I was now living with—also had it.

My dad opened the front door, and we squeezed in one at a time. In the entryway, there were a few cubby shelves and three hooks for coats. Next to that was a sofa. On the opposite wall, a woodburning stove, no bigger than my childhood Easy-Bake Oven, took up most of the space.

"Here's the kitchen," my dad said, officiating the tour. The kitchen was better referenced as two cabinets with a counter bolted to the top of them. "Is that a fridge?" I pointed to the only normal-sized appliance in the room.

"It is. We realized it would be nice to have some of the comforts we were accustomed to, so we're going to use solar to supply energy to that fridge. We have solar energy for a few luxuries." He said the word luxuries like we were staying at the Ritz Carlton.

"Do we get real lights?" I half joked but stiffened, terrified of the answer.

"We have lights wired into the house, but we probably won't have the solar energy to run them all the time, especially if there is daylight we can use. We did also splurge on a small water heater for the shower."

Shower. My dad had said the most miraculous word, and I finally had a tiny ray of hope.

"Speaking of which . . ." He opened a door at the back of the kitchen. "Here's the bathroom. We need to supply and filter our own water up here, but unfortunately, we don't have a well drilled yet. We are waiting on the permit. We are hoping to get it this month, but until then we must haul in all the water. To make the workload less, we'll ration it. I figured if we each take a ten-minute shower every other day, we should be okay for now."

I was learning to let his words go in one ear and slide right over and out the other ear without having to digest them, because the more I heard, the worse my life became.

"And this little baby over here"—he pointed to a bucket with a lid in the corner of the bathroom—"is our very own composting toilet. Best system around."

I groaned and backed out of the room. Upcycling human waste! I couldn't take it anymore, but I held my tongue because I knew no one cared.

My dad opened another door next to the bathroom. "This is our room." I peeked in and realized by room he meant microscopic storage area that they would be sleeping in. "And," he said as he pointed to the ceiling, "I saved the best for last. These stairs lead up to your loft." He motioned to what I thought was a bookcase, but it was cubicle shelves that stacked in ascending order against the wall. My eyes followed the pattern to see a loft suspended from the A-frame ceiling, reminiscent of how spiders lived unnoticed and tucked in a corner. I forced a weak smile. I couldn't have been offered a private loft at a better time. I needed to get away from this reality. My dad helped me to saddle my dance bag on my shoulder and I ascended the stairs, weighed down with the entire contents of my city life.

My loft had a platform bed and a shelf on the wall above it. Two drawers were tucked into the bottom of the bed. The crowning feature was the octagon-shaped window above the head of my bed. I ducked down to crawl across the bed over to the window.

An intimidatingly huge mountain loomed outside of my window. Evergreen trees dotted the surface in an endless spiral to the sky. I bowed my head, trying to see the top of the mountain, but it was lost in the clouds. I let my eyes drop to the valley, where I saw the Rogers' home. I closed my eyes, imagining when I opened them again that I would see a city skyline and a coffee shop. Or maybe the ocean. Then I opened my eyes and cringed. It didn't work.

Chapter Six

The next morning, I cupped my mug of coffee with both of my hands and stood on the tiny porch, wondering what I was supposed to do all day. There was no way people had fun out in the middle of nowhere. I leaned against the porch rail, looking out at the never-ending nothingness with my lips pulling into an even deeper frown.

"Don't try to go exploring by yourself," my dad walked up beside me and warned me casually as if I was wanting to converse. Apparently in the last month, he had taken to wearing jeans and flannel. It was such a drastic change from his pressed dressed shirts, I still found myself staring at him, wondering where my old dad went. "This area's known for bears."

"So, I need to have someone I can outrun tag along with me."

"Have someone go along with you who has a loaded weapon," Eddie corrected me from where he stood across the yard. I didn't even know he could hear me way over there. Apparently, he had no shame in listening to my conversations or giving unsolicited advice.

"I carry my pistol everywhere when I'm outside. I asked Fulton to do the same."

"Isn't that why they make bear spray?" I asked, not sure I wanted anything to do with guns.

"That can't hurt. Bring that too. Just make sure when you're outside you're prepared. Be watching." My dad handed me a metal bucket and continued to stare at me as if he was waiting for a reaction.

Since he didn't bother to explain, I raised a quizzical eyebrow in his direction. "What's this for?"

"It's gathering time."

I understood exactly what he meant, but there was no way I was letting him end this conversation so easily. "Huh?"

"We can't sit here all day like it's an unending coffee break." He pushed the bucket closer to me, but I didn't move an inch to take it. With frustration in his breath, he carried on, "We only have a few months to get everything together before winter. Eddie said there's a bunch of ripe choke cherry bushes on the other side of the stream. We need to gather them to preserve."

"Can't we just buy them at the store?" I huffed with my hand on my hip, not wanting anything to do with chores. When no one answered me, I added, "I'm sure they go on sale for like a dollar or two."

Laughter rose from the animal pen, and my dad looked over and said, "Looks like you have a volunteer partner."

Fulton stood up from where he had been hunched over, filling feed buckets. "I guess I can go with her." He tried to brush the dirt off the knees of his jeans, but it only revealed another darker layer of dirt. "I did tell Millie I would take her to the stream to pick sweet pea flowers. Might as well bring her now too." He walked over to his house, opened the screen door, and called in, "Millie, time to get your flowers." He let the door slam and retrieved a small wagon that was parked next to the house. As he pulled it toward me, he asked, "You ready?" His light green eyes struck me as unusually cheerful for being on their way to do manual labor.

"No," I grumble through gritted teeth

The way he smirked showed obvious signs he was holding back a chuckle. "Me neither."

Millie ran out of the house, her caramel-colored pigtails bouncing. She was swinging a flat, white wicker basket by her side. Fulton took her basket and threw it into the wagon. Then we left together with Millie dancing through the meadows like she was auditioning for a Mary Poppins movie. Fulton and I trudged behind her as if we were walking through tar pits.

"How come I can't feel like that?" I pointed to Millie, who had just completed a decent cartwheel. "I feel like someone died."

"I can tell you're taking this the hardest."

"How are you not?" I searched his face for any signs of agony, but he looked alarmedly content.

"Honestly, the way I see it, I turn eighteen two weeks after school starts. I talked to a buddy back home, and his parents said I can come live with them to finish out the school year."

I furrowed my eyebrows. "Wait. You get to leave?"

"They can't keep me here. It's like a bad summer camp for me, and then I'm out."

"Lucky." I immediately started to add up the months until I turned eighteen. "I have almost twenty months. Unless . . . do you think they'll quit this farming thing before then?"

"Is that a serious question?"

"I guess not."

He stared off in the distance. "Twenty months can't be too bad."

"It's a death sentence."

He pointed to bushes across the stream. "Those are the fullest. Millie and I already picked all the berries on this side last week. We can cross the water over there where it's shallow."

I followed them, copying what they did. They took off their shoes and rolled up their pant legs. I waded my way through the water after them, bucket under my arm. "Brrr, that's the coldest water I've ever walked through." Back on solid ground, I hopped lightly on my toes, hoping to get the blood flowing to bring warmth back to my feet.

"It's fresh thaw." Fulton pointed toward the mountain in the distance with a snowcap covering the tip of it. "That's where the stream comes from. This is some of the cleanest water you'll ever see. That's what makes the berries so juicy." He popped one into his mouth. "There are huckleberry bushes down that way. I've never tried one before, but apparently, they are supposed to be amazing. This part of Montana is known for them. They won't be ripened until fall, though."

"When did you become an expert in berries?" I dropped my bucket on the ground and started harvesting the same bush.

He gave me a suspicious look and kept picking berries. Millie crouched and picked from the lower branches while we cleaned off the top.

"You don't know?" I asked after a few minutes passed with no reply.

He scratched the back of his head like he had one of those itches that were painful. "I thought you were being sarcastic. I didn't see the point of answering when I figured you didn't actually care."

"What does that mean?"

"Nothing." He lowered his eyes back to the bush.

Annoyed at how difficult Fulton was being, I shifted my attention to Millie, who was filling her mouth with more berries than she had put in the bucket. "You like this new life?" I asked.

"I love it. Mom and Dad are bringing goats home tonight. I get to help milk them."

My nose wrinkled at the thought. "You like all these animals you get to have for pets then?"

"Mom said if I take good care of them, I can get more, and I can have a whole petting zoo that can be my business to take to schools and fairs and birthday parties. Next, I want to get bunnies."

"A business," I echoed. "Isn't there a rule against child labor?" I checked my bucket, hoping to be almost done, but the bottom wasn't even covered with one layer yet.

Fulton looked at me while he picked. "It's all part of the living-off-the-land plan. My parents think this is a great opportunity to learn business skills as well as survival skills."

I rudely chuckled.

"Just wait. Your parents feel the same way. They haven't told you about it yet because you've been such a grump."

I let my hand hover over my bucket. "How am I supposed to act?"

"Never mind." He lowered his eyes to the bush again.

"No, it means something." I glared at him. "What are you talking about?"

"It's just how you are to people."

"How is that?" I could feel the stress lines in my forehead creasing with annoyance.

"Forget it." He started pulling berries off the bush a little more forcefully than he had been a few minutes earlier.

"If something's on your mind, you might as well say it. It's not like we're going to be able to hide from each other here." I squared my body, facing him.

"I hesitate to say it because I know you won't listen to anything I say, but you're not the only person who doesn't want to be here." His brief glance in my direction before returning to his diligent work was just enough to annoy me even more.

"And your point?" I rested one hand on my hip.

"You act like it's all about you, and like you're too good for everything."

"What do you expect? I was ripped away from my whole life." My voice raised a notch. "I'm not okay with it, and I can't pretend to be."

Millie raised her crystal-blue eyes to plead with me. "Don't be mad. He's just trying to help."

I ignored her comment and refocused on Fulton, who had stopped working and now stood with an exasperated look on his face. He said, "Look, I'm only the messenger, but it's not just about the move. That's how you were in New York too."

"Are you saying I'm mean?"

"All I'm saying is you have a chance to start over here. Do you want to be the same girl you were there?"

I huffed in dismay. "Who am I supposed to be if I can't be me?"

"You can decide to be who you want to be, but I remember who you were before you went to your private school, and that girl was at least nice. You can't stand there and tell me you didn't know you had a mean-girl reputation."

"The people who said that were jealous."

He stretched to pick a clump of berries toward the back of the bush. I thought he wasn't going to answer, but after a while he said in a soft voice, "It's all a matter of perception." We didn't talk anymore after that.

The sun beat down on our heads, making my forehead bead with sweat. I wasn't getting much done, as I kept having to stop every few minutes to swat flies away. It was an exercise in patience to have to fill a bucket with tiny berries one by one, but it was even harder trying to ignore someone when you were harvesting berries from the same bush.

After the bucket was full, we slogged back down the path to the stream. I rolled my pants up past my knees to wade back across it. I walked slowly, adjusting to the cold. I was getting my rhythm and then I slipped. My bucket tipped and I watched as several berries rolled out and fell into the water. I planted my feet on the ground but at the same time felt something poke and snag the back of my jeans.

I placed my foot out to step, but I was stuck. I felt behind me and discovered a branch from a sunken tree had snagged my jeans. I slid my thumb inside the hole, ripping it bigger to release the branch's hold until I was free. "I just ripped a three-hundred-dollar pair of jeans!" I cried out.

Fulton's head flew back as he laughed.

"And I'm cold!" I took short, fast steps out of the water. On land, our wagon was parked waiting for us. I hobbled over to check it, wishing for a towel. Nothing.

"Did you step on something?" Fulton asked as he released Millie's hold, allowing her to slide down his back.

"You okay?" Millie asked, running over to me.

"Just mad. My stupid ankle made me tip over in the strong current. I can't believe I dumped all those berries. That was like an hour of work."

"I thought you were supposed to get your ankles fixed," Fulton said.

"I was going to, but the doctor refused unless I stopped dancing."

Fulton gave me a confused look before adding, "Cause you're dancing so much now . . ."

"Right." I winced from the unignorable pain that bolted through my ankle when I tried to step. Fighting tears, I looked back at Fulton. His neck and ears had a fresh reddened layer over what had been sun-bronzed skin. The ends of his short tawny hair plastered to his head like sticky noodles. I knew he was exhausted, but I didn't have another option. "You're going to have to give me a ride," I said in a tiny voice.

I thought he would tell me to get lost, but then he offered me a weary smile and nodded toward the wagon. "Get in." I sat in the wagon and balanced a bucket on top of my lap as we rode back in silence to the farm.

"Day one and already a casualty," my dad said when he saw Fulton wheeling me into the yard. I had been letting my attitude fester the whole way back and my mood had plummeted even more. When I didn't say anything because I didn't want to have to admit my attitude problem, my dad asked, "What happened?" He held out his hand to help me up, but I pushed it away.

"You won," I stated firmly after I pulled myself up. I limped to the door and opened it. "I'll have the stupid surgery." I slammed the door behind me and crawled on my knees up the stairs to get to my loft. Humiliation had flooded in my chest, making it hard to breathe, and I'd never wanted to run away from anywhere more than I did right now.

Running away wasn't an option.

Instead, I hung my head and sobbed.

Chapter Seven

Later that afternoon, I woke from a hard nap. With my mind still loitering between dreamland and reality, I could already tell my ankle had puffed up like a Pillsbury biscuit. I knew I should've iced it, but only civilized people have access to ice. I would have had to drill a hole in the ground, hoping I could reach all the way to Antarctica to grab a chunk and tie it with the golden string that I magically grew out of my butt and then have my unicorn pull it back! I sighed to myself. Okay, that was a little overdramatic, but I had reasons for my attitude.

I sat up with a scowl on my face. My body felt tacky, but unlucky for me it wasn't my day to shower. I leaned to look out my window and spotted that the goats had arrived. Millie was luring one to her with fresh alfalfa. My airway got tight when I realized I knew what alfalfa was. This was not my life!

Dad and Fulton were digging a ginormous pit for a root cellar. They were smiling, which annoyed me. Then I remember how I had spoken to Fulton before he ended up wheeling me all the way home. I know I would never have helped someone who had just told me off. If I was truly honest with myself, I knew if I had been Fulton, I would have left me there to limp home on my own. For the briefest of moments, I felt guilty about how I treated Fulton. I had been horrible to him.

I hobbled down the stairs and went outside. Everyone greeted me with a smile, but it was different this time. I knew I didn't deserve those smiles. "I don't think this will surprise you," my dad said, "but you're officially demoted from gatherer." He wrapped his arm around my shoulder. "You okay?" He looked at my bulging ankle and then met my eyes with concern.

"It hurts, but I'm more mad than anything." I stared forward as if I was gaining strength by not making eye contact.

"What are you mad about?" He shifted his weight from one foot to the next. I started to think he really didn't want to talk to me anymore than I wanted to talk to him, but he kept on, adding, "It was an accident."

"Well, for starters, I tore my favorite jeans."

"I thought ripped jeans were in style?" His rebuttal was given in a even tone, but I didn't even try to match it.

"They ripped out the butt," I said, rolling my eyes.

"We could sew a bear trap flap on there." He grinned a good-natured smile, and I could see he was doing his best to get me to smile, but I wasn't giving in.

I gave him my unamused straight smile. "Funny."

"No, he's right." Linda spoke up from her spot in front of her house. I was completely startled. I hadn't realized she was standing over there. Once again, I was reminded that there is no such thing as privacy on this homestead. Every conversation I have, someone is waiting to chime in. She continues, unashamed that she was listening, "I can teach you how to put a patch on them."

"A patch on my butt?" How I managed to say that with a straight face is beyond me. Did she hear herself?

Linda shrugged her thick shoulders, as she took a moment to wipe her hands off on the work apron she always wore. "We could try."

"You should let her teach you," my dad said. I guess I needed to add another person to intrude on my conversations.

I wanted to tell him what a dumb idea that was, but I did only have a few pairs of pants, and my live-off-the-land parents were not going to let me shop. Fulton's words about how I treated people rung in my ears. I decided if I wanted to change how I was, I needed to start with small gestures. I forced my lips to curl over my gritted teeth. "Sure, we could try. Thanks for offering."

"I think it would be fun." She smiled back at me like she was about to tell me the sweetest secret. "Give yourself a few days to heal, and when you're ready, come on over."

I watched her stir something inside a small bucket. Part of me knew I should ask if she needed help, but I was tired, and I didn't want to work. I hated this. So instead of offering to help, I asked, "What are you working on?"

"I'm making ice cream from Millie's first batch of goat's milk."

"That sounds like a treat." My mouth watered at the word ice cream even if the word *goat* was attached to it.

"That's what I thought. We need a treat to celebrate our first full day of being together. It just needs a little more stirring before it's ready." She looked content when she stirred, but it jabbed at my heart. This was her forever dream, but it was killing me. Again, I felt like I should offer to help her, but I stubbornly looked away.

Fulton was now digging the pit alone. The deepening pit flashed in front of my face as the perfect metaphor for how my life was going. I dragged my bum foot across the yard. Apparently, I'm terrible at that too because I didn't notice that I was traipsing all over the marigolds my mom had just carefully planted to try to keep the mosquitos away. I quickly apologized to my mom and continued to drag myself in Fulton's direction.

"Hey," I called over to Fulton. The tone in my voice came out more like a rescue call than a friendly gesture.

"Hey." He kept his eyes on his shoveling. I get he thought I was here to be annoying. I waited for him to lift a huge shovel full of dirt out of the way before I tried again.

"Can we talk?" I tilted my head to the side, trying to get a better view of his expression. Maybe it was just my imagination, but he seemed to turn his head away from me.

"Talk?" One of his eyebrows rose up, as if that's all I needed for an invitation to pour my heart out. I wanted him to at least look at me.

"Please," I added, careful to sound friendly this time.

He finally turned, revealing a thin sheen of sweat framed on one side of his face. With his shovel still in hand, he stood silently.

I shrugged my shoulders, hoping it would help the words to come easy, but they didn't budge. All I could manage was, "Sorry."

"It's okay," he snorted through his reply, making it clear he didn't consider my apology genuine.

"And thank you," I rushed the last part out like the words were made of fire and they hurt to hold in my mouth.

I was hoping that would be enough, and I slide one foot back. The pain was unbearable, and it halted me right as he tacked on, "For what?"

Resisting the urge to glare at him, I lifted one side of my lips into a lopsided grin as that's all I had to give. He knew what I was apologizing for. The fact he was acting this way annoyed me, but I pushed through it. "For not leaving me there for bear food."

He wiped his temple with the back of his hand while he kept his serious expression. "How's your foot?"

"Awesome." I was proud of all the sass I mustered up.

"Is that what that giant lump on your ankle is called?"

I gave him a thumbs up. "Yep. Awesome with a little bit of sass."

His lips curled into a half-grin, challenging me. "Just a little bit of sass?"

"Yep." I pinched my lips together, unwilling to admit to anything more.

"Well, I'm glad it's just a little bit. I wouldn't want to see you go full throttle."

I wasn't sure what else I would say in my half-hearted apology, so I was thankful when Linda's voice broke the air in between us. "Hey, you guys want ice cream? It's done."

Fulton stabbed his shovel into the ground and waved at his mom. When I turned to hop back, I felt his arm wrap around my waist, helping to pull me forward. At first, I froze. I wasn't sure if I'd ever allowed Fulton to wrap his arm around me before. This certainly wasn't something I had on my Bingo card for this year. Come on, gimpy," his voice was teasing, but the tender way he nudged me forward was more than a little confusing. He was being my friend.

Against all my sudden instincts, I allowed myself to lean on his arm for support. Oddly, I didn't hate the help. My foot didn't want any pressure added to it, and after trying and failing for the second time, I mumbled, "I hate this."

"I know." That's all he said, but he stayed by me until I was back to my front porch where everyone else was already eating their dessert.

"It may sound sort of gross being that it's goat milk, but I added tons of vanilla and sugar, and I think it's pretty tasty," Linda said. I cupped the bowl she handed me, letting my hands absorb the coolness. "Do you want syrup?" she asked. "I made some from those berries you guys brought back."

"I almost died getting those berries, so you bet I'm going to eat them." I held my bowl up for her. With a spoon, she drizzled a stream of syrup over my ice cream. A dab of it dripped over the side of my bowl, and I leaned over to lick it. I let the stickiness roll over my tongue. It was tart, yet sweet.

"How is it?" she asked as she stood back with one hand on her hip, fully ready to accept compliments.

"Really good," I didn't hold back my true feelings. "But so not worth all that work. I seriously think this stuff goes on sale for a couple bucks at the store." Everyone politely laughed. I looked around at them all smiling and enjoying themselves, and it hurt because I felt so left out of their excitement. I could not be happy about any of this.

I can't even be happy about the ice cream.

Chapter Eight

The next morning, I stiffly sipped my coffee while my mom sat across from me. It felt awkward. I couldn't remember ever having a morning when my mom hung out and drank coffee with me. Part of me was still paranoid about her fuzzy unibrow, but I was yet to see it since we left the city.

"Your dad left for town already," she spoke without looking over at me. "It's supposed to rain today, and he wanted to get some supplies for the well. He got the permit to dig it. A guy's coming later this week to help him."

"Oh." My eyes landed on her side profile. Her mellow blonde hair had been combed into a low ponytail, and only a few crow's feet peeked out from her makeup-free face. I could see how she could have been pretty in her youth. Truthfully, she would be pretty now if she didn't always have her unibrow simmering, waiting for the moment that her internal heat built up enough pressure to boil over and throb it at me.

"He said when he's in town he'd try to make you a doctor appointment for your ankle." How her voice can say that sentence and lack compassion will always amaze me.

"Okay." I watched the lines by her mouth. I wanted them to soften and turn up, even if it was just the slightest, tiniest bit to tell me surgery was going to be fine, but they didn't waver. "I probably should have already had it taken care of by now." My voice hinted at a vulnerability I never let her see.

"It's fine." She turned her head away from me and stood up. "I could use a refill. Do you need one?"

"Nah." I longingly looked down into my empty cup. I wanted to have another cup of coffee with my mom. I desperately wanted to tell her all about how bad my ankle hurt, how much I missed my friends, and how I even started to feel a little sorry about the way I had been acting, but I knew better. That wasn't what my mom and I did. I also stood, stretching my arms above my head. "I think I'll go see if Linda can help me fix my pants."

My mom raised an eyebrow at me, which suddenly made me self-conscious.

"I mean, since it's going to rain today . . ." I stared back at her, wondering if I'd had made her jealous by wanting to go to Linda's. That thought lasted all of two seconds, though, because she disappeared into the bathroom without a word.

Without help, I hopped across the yard to Linda's house. Before I could knock, Fulton opened the porch door. "Were you just sitting there and watching out the window?" I asked when I passed through the open door into their screened-in porch.

"Where else am I supposed to sit?" He closed the door behind me.

"In your room."

"This is my room."

"You're living on your porch?"

His facial expression sarcastically told me life just kept getting better. "I was supposed to sleep on the couch, but I missed the privacy of my own room, so I moved a recliner out here." He motioned to the chair squeezed in the corner that would obviously only be able to recline when someone wasn't standing where I was standing.

I did a fast eye sweep of the porch and felt sorry for him. "Don't you feel like a caged animal?"

"Don't you?" One of his eyebrows quirked above the other, adding to the pointed look he was giving me.

"Good point." I eyed the flimsy porch screens. "What are you going to do when winter comes?"

His eyes told me I knew the answer to my question.

"Right." I injected a point-making finger in the air between us. "You're not going to be here."

With a finger held up to his lips, he whispered, "Don't say anything."

"I won't," I whispered, matching his volume.

"Thank you."

On the floor, a stack of books leaned against his chair. Turning my head sideways, I read one of the book spines. "Animal husbandry. That has to be entertaining," I teased. When he didn't say anything, I added, "You're getting into this animal thing, aren't you?"

"I've always liked animals."

"There's a difference between liking animals and studying animal husbandry."

"It's something to do." He shrugged his bony shoulders. "Plus, I like the way they communicate without words. I love when they have that moment of recognition, and you can see it in their eyes that they trust you."

"I usually can't get past the smell." My joke fell flat as Fulton simply motioned to the door.

"You can go inside," he said and opened the door for me. Their tiny home had the same layout as ours. The only real difference was that they had squeezed in a full-sized dining table, which took up most of the middle of the room. Millie's bare feet hung down over my head from where she was sitting in her loft. A few weeks ago, this scene would have horrified me, but today I found it almost normal.

"Come sit, Abs." Linda motioned to a wooden chair at the table. "Let me grab my sewing basket." She disappeared into the bedroom, and I was left looking at Millie's swinging legs.

"How do you like your loft?" I called up to her.

"I love it. I can see the whole world from up here."

"The whole world? That's a pretty good view."

"Yep. Did you see my chickens?" The excitement in her voice ticked up.

"I did not. I didn't know you had any."

"They're in the shower. Go look." She pointed to a door in the exact location as our bathroom. I considered that an invitation and slid my feet in that direction.

I cracked the door. Sure enough, their bathtub was filled with about a dozen yellow and tan fuzzy chicks sleeping under a light.

"Cute little things." I shut the door quickly because the smell was actually quite pungent. "Why are they in there?"

"Fulton brought them in out of the rain because they needed to stay warm." I arched my chin up to listen as it was sort of hard to hear her from up there. "We didn't have anywhere to put a tub of chickens, so that's where they are until they go outside."

Linda returned, setting her wicker basket on the table, and she patted the seat next to her. "Sit, dear." I obeyed, moving closer to her while she spoke, "Have you ever sewed anything?"

"Nope." I popped the p on the end of my word and stared at her sewing basket that was so crammed full of fabric, and spools of thread. I was instantly overwhelmed.

She rummaged through the top tray of her basket, letting the silence expand for just a moment before she produced a needle, and said, "Then we'll start with the basics." With the needle in one hand and a string of thread in the other, she instructed, "This is how you thread the needle." She twisted the end of the thread into a point and effortlessly slipped it through the needle eye. "Then you tie a knot at the end, and you are ready to sew." She handed me the needle, and she reached over to grab my pants. "Well, look at that," she blurted out when she saw the gaping hole in my butt. "That'll get you some attention."

"That's not the attention I need." Despite my best effort not to enjoy this, my lips curled up. "Can we rescue them?"

"Sure." She ran her fingers along the middle seam. "This seam can be mended back together, and you won't even notice it was ever torn." She moved her fingers up along the top of the opening. "But this part here is too thin to mend. That's because it frayed when it tore, see that?" She pinched her fingers around the hole.

"Yeah. So, what do we do?" I pretend to care more about this project than I actually do. She's just being so nice, and I would hate for her to know how boring this was to me.

"That's where we'll put the patch." She held it further out in front of her. "Actually, that might look sort of cute if we find the right shape. What color do you want?" She lifted the tray out of her basket and pulled out a small stack of brightly colored fabric patches from the bottom compartment.

I frowned, unable to spare my true feelings. "I'm not really sure I want a bright color on my butt. Isn't that worse than a hole?"

"I know what we can use." She went back into the bedroom and came back with a plastic bag. "I was saving this to make some new things for Millie once she got done with her summer growth, but it won't hurt to snip off a little corner." Holding the bag with one hand, she pulled out the end of the fabric with the other. "It's aubergine!" She gleamed, holding up the purple fabric.

"Of course it is." I forced a smile, unsure where I would ever wear jeans with a purple butt. Wishing I had thrown them away to save us both from wasting a whole morning, I tried to come up with the words to tell her not to bother, but it was evident by her bright smile that she was enjoying the project.

"Now, what shape should we make?" She took a step back to study the project. "It needs to be something fun since it's on the top of your butt. What do you want to sit on?"

I don't even know any shapes. It's not like math was ever my thing. I settle on something easy, and say, "A heart?"

Her smile straightened but her eyes never lost the glean in them. "You can't sit on a heart. That's bad luck for love."

"I don't know then." I shrugged, still not enjoying this project half as much as she was. "I was trying to think of something easy to make because I don't know how to make any shapes."

Her lips purse to the side for a beat. "How 'bout a pair of ballet slippers? We could cut out the silhouette of the shoes, and they can be sewn here." She drew a circle around the hole with her finger. "Then, we could take embroidery thread to add details like the laces. If we want to be fancy, we could make the laces wrap up this way, and they could actually help hide where this is torn." She traced the bottom of the waistline.

"We could try." It looked like way more work than I wanted to do, but again I was trying to not act rude.

"It's not like you're going to wear them this way anyway." She dug through her basket, finding scissors and set them aside for easy access.

"Right." I leaned forward and watched her work, trying to lend my hand when I knew I wouldn't be totally destructive. I wouldn't say I enjoyed it, but time didn't seem to stand still. I was actually almost not miserable. I smiled when we were done. Mostly, I smiled because were done. However, a tiny part of that smile was because I had accomplished something. Well, actually two things: salvaging my pants and improving my attitude. I never thought either would happen.

It was a start.

Chapter Nine

The beautiful thing about needing ankle surgery when you live in the brush is you must go to a real city to have it. A couple weeks had passed, and it was the morning of my surgery. I needed to be checked into the hospital by six, and I was nervous as I descended the bookcase stairs on my butt. My sprain had healed weeks ago, but I wasn't taking any chances. I was about to plop down on the couch to wait for my dad when he flew in from outside. "Something's up with the water pump we just put in."

"What?" I heard him, but it was more my disbelief that made me question.

"The yard's flooded with water. I'm not sure if a pipe cracked or what. I shut off the pump so it won't run anymore, but I can't leave it like this. Mom's going to have to take you in for your surgery." My dad disappeared into their room. I heard muffled voices for several minutes. Then my dad returned, barely looking at me. "Sorry, Abs, Mom has a headache. She can't drive. But come to think about it, you're all pre-registered for the surgery. Would you be okay if Linda or someone else drove you?"

"Seriously?" My outburst was instant, and then I lowered my brows in disgust. "I'm having surgery."

"You know how your mom gets." My dad's overly forced neutral tone revealed he was also saddened by my mom's timing, and I knew there was nothing either one of us could do.

"Whatever. Let's just get this over with," I muttered.

"I'll go see who's awake." He hustled out the front door. The house got abnormally quiet when I was left alone with my thoughts. I stared at my mom's closed bedroom door. On a different planet, I would have been able to run right into an inviting hug. She would smooth my hair back, telling me my surgery was going to be fine, that I was strong, and there was nothing to worry about. *But that wasn't my planet.*

"Abs," my dad whispered from the open door. "Fulton's got the truck running. Come out when you are ready."

Being pawned off on Fulton gave me a hollowness in my heart. It didn't bother me that my dad had an emergency chore he needed to tend to, but my mom always did this to me. I slowly trudged out the door and kept my chin tucked when I climbed into my dad's truck. Part of me was relieved to see Millie sitting next to Fulton in the truck, and I smiled weakly at her. "Morning," I said, still refusing to smile.

"Morning," Fulton said with the biggest grin I'd seen on him since we moved.

"Why are you so happy?" I asked.

"Your dad pounded on my door and said I could have a day lying around in air conditioning with unlimited TV, and he offered me fifty bucks for food. It's like Christmas morning."

"My dad's the best marketer in the world." Shaking my head, I cross my hands over my chest and slump way down in my seat. "I should've known he'd spin taking me to the hospital as something fun."

"When Millie heard there'd be television, she jumped in the truck too."

Millie beamed sweetly at me. Maybe it was their innocence of wanting to see a stupid screen, or maybe it was because I was suddenly relieved to have a day of freedom from my parents, but the nerves I had been feeling simmered down. I flashed a genuine grin back at Millie. "When I went in for my pre-op, I saw a huge TV in the waiting room."

"I don't even think my eyes will be able to handle the glories of TV anymore," she joked while her beautiful blue eyes sparkled all her joy.

"I know, right?" I managed to playfully tap her elbow with mine as my mood was lifting a little.

"Let's get this truck moving," Millie commanded by pointing her finger forward.

Fulton put the truck in gear and said, "We are off."

Millie cheered and out of my side-eye I could see both of their smiles. Maybe I am a grump, but I just don't have a reason to smile today. As we drove down the gravel road, I thought what it would be like to be in town without my dad. "It would be nice to call someone back home," I thought out loud. "I haven't talked to anyone since we left. It feels like a million years ago, not just a month. Have either of you talked to anyone from back home?"

Fulton shook his head. "Nope. All my ties to normalness are gone."

The anticipation of civilization was building, and all I could think about was getting to use technology. I had forgotten about my surgery and was now just excited to be off the farm without my parents. "Thank the Lord for a broken water pump," I said after many long beats of silence.

Fulton looked at me while flashing me his mischievous smirk. "Did you break it?"

"I wish." I blew out a heavy breath as I could just imagine all the trouble I'd get in if I had broken it.

He let out a good-natured chuckle. "Come on. You mean this wasn't part of your master plan to bust off the land?"

"If it were, I'd have something more fun lined up than a surgery."

"Right. Oh, I forgot." He pointed to two travel mugs sitting in the cup holders. "My mom sent coffee for us if you want some."

I lifted my mug and inhaled the much-appreciated smell. "That smells amazing, but I can't eat or drink anything before surgery. Not even water." I sighed loudly. "Now I'm bummed." I replaced the mug in the cup holder, letting my mind linger on the deliciousness contained inside.

"Bummer for you. Good for me. Guess I'll have to drink yours too."

"That was sweet of your mom though. She loves this homesteading thing, doesn't she?" My eyes followed the sun rays cresting our mountain. They cast a morning glow on everything in its path, including a row of newly blooming lilac bushes that, for the moments when the sun kissed them, sparkled with golden flecks. It truly was breathtaking, but it didn't soothe me in the way that it should. It still didn't feel like home here. If anything, I felt like I was in the longest nightmare ever.

"She loves the mom things." Fulton steered the truck around the bend in the road. "She loves taking care of people. I think she's worried about your surgery, too." From the corner of my eye, I saw Fulton stole a peek at me.

"My mom didn't even come out to say hello to me this morning." My statement hung in the air, and it lowered the mood in the truck. I regretted blurting that out, but it was the truth, and I couldn't change it.

"I think she does the best that she knows how," Fulton added after the silence had become uncomfortable.

I swallowed, feeling a lump that hadn't been there earlier. That was probably the most honest thing anyone had ever said about my mom.

Fulton took a slow sip of coffee like it would wash away this conversation, and then he turned the radio on. "We should be able to get something on here now that we're closer to town."

"Yes, music. Let's get this road trip started." I forced a happy voice, but after a while of listening to music and joking with Fulton and Millie, I was surprisingly in a better mood.

We pulled into the hospital parking lot and filed out of the truck toward the hospital entrance. I looked back at my dad's rusted frog truck, caked in mud from the days in the fields. "You know, it's strange how the first time my dad made me ride in that truck, I was petrified someone would see me. But today I couldn't care less if someone saw me get out of it. I feel like the luckiest girl."

"A lot has changed since then." Fulton held the entrance door open and waited for me to walk through it. "And this time you got to ride in it with us."

"Is that why?" I slid in front of him and waited for Millie to catch up.

Millie grabbed my hand long enough to cut in front of me as we passed through the door. "I love riding in that truck. It brought us to TV land." She darted through the second set of doors and plopped down in front of the waiting room television.

"I don't think she even knows what she's watching," Fulton said as he walked to the receptionist line with me.

"I don't think it matters," I said. I didn't feel the least bit confused by her behavior. Inside, I was bubbling with excitement to see something on the screen. Anything that would connect me to society.

"I think I could watch the static channel and be perfectly content."

"Anything would be great." I shuffled my feet forward to the front of the line, and I handed my insurance card to the gal at the desk. "Aubergine White checking in."

"That's a gorgeous name," the receptionist replied with her gaze fixed on my card.

"Thanks. My dad likes it."

"And, let me check here." She moved to her computer and typed something on her keyboard, before finishing her sentence, "You're here for surgery this morning, correct?"

"Yes." I'm not one to have a nervous fidget, but I've also never had surgery before, and I found myself chewing on the inside of my cheek.

"You are pre-registered." She nodded to herself after checking on her computer screen again. "I already have your insurance information, so I don't need your cards. And who do you have with you today that we need to notify of updates?"

"Um, my friend." I motioned to Fulton and then trapped my lip in my teeth.

"Great, you can add him to your HIPPA form." She slipped a sheet of paper to me, and I scribbled on it, adding Fulton's name. "Thank you," she said and then pointed forward. "You may go down this corridor and take a left into that waiting area. A nurse will take you back when they are ready. Oh, and here is your surgery I.D. number." She flashed a yellow card with the number four on it at me and then handed it to Fulton. "There's a television screen in the waiting area that has all the patients' numbers on it," she said to him, "and it will keep you updated by letting you know when she goes in and gets out of surgery, so watch for that." She turned back to me. "This is your I.D. bracelet. Check your name and your birthday."

"Looks good." I held out my wrist for her to attach the bracelet for me.

"You're all set. Have a nice day." She smiled sweetly at me. My stomach looped into a bundle of knots. Things were getting real. It was time to head back. Fulton walked close to me, and he managed to speak softly without Millie hearing, "I'm finding this a little awkward that I'm the person who gets notified if something goes drastically wrong."

I cringed. I had hoped he wouldn't pick up on that. "I was hoping you wouldn't bring that up."

"Why?" His voice was even quieter.

"It's super embarrassing that you have to do any of this." The backs of my eyes stung with tears. I was fine with my mom ditching me. I was used to that, but having to go through all of this in front of Fulton was another level of humiliation.

"But do you think it's odd your parents aren't here?" I made the mistake of looking up at him, and he caught me in a look with his brows raised in concern, and they seemed to hold a power to prevent me from looking away.

After a long beat, I managed to break our eye contact, and I lowered my gaze to watch my feet as we walked. "I'm used to it."

"If you would have told me a year ago that I would be the person to notify of your medical status while you're in surgery, I would never have believed it." I could tell by the way he added a humor inflection to his voice that he was trying to cheer me up, but I was honestly just so sick of all of this.

"I wouldn't have believed any part of my current life," I murmured to myself as we walked the rest of the hallway and found chairs in the new waiting area. Millie quickly discovered a game tablet that she coveted in the corner, and we all fell into a stony silence.

It wasn't long before a nurse appeared in the opened door and called, "Aubergine White."

I stood and replied, "That's me." I looked back at Fulton, and if I didn't know him better, I would think he looked a little nervous as his gaze bounced from me to the nurse and back again.

"Good luck," he finally offered with an unconvincing shrug.

"Thanks." I started to slide my feet forward, but then I turned back. I couldn't leave things like that. "Fulton."

His eyes lit up, focusing on me.

"I know this is weird for both of us." I pulled my lips into a lopsided half-grin. "I appreciate it."

He gave a slight nod of his head with the most serious expression I've seen him have in a long time. "It's our pleasure, right, Millie?" he said while giving her a jab of his elbow.

Millie looked up from her tablet like she had forgotten there were other people in existence. "Yeah, it's awesome."

I giggled a little at Millie's cuteness, and then I pivoted to follow the nurse. It wasn't ever going to be perfect, not even close, but I would make it through this.

Chapter Ten

After surgery, I was moved to my recovery room. As I became more aware, I could feel a warm body next to me. My eyes blinked open to find Millie snuggled next to me in my bed, with her eyes zeroed in on the TV.

"You always snuggle random unconscious people?" I ask, my voice raspy.

She smiled innocently back at me. "I wanted to get the best view, and you were in my way."

"Sorry that my inability to move was an inconvenience to your show," I said with not even a hint of sarcasm because I found her actions insanely cute.

"You're such a turd, Millie," Fulton said from the corner chair. "I told her not to sit there, but she's a serial snuggler."

"A serial snuggler?" I raised an eyebrow back at Millie. "That sounds serious."

"I love to snuggle." Mille wiggled next to me like she was trying to snuggle deeper. "But only with people I love."

Millie, admitting to me so casually that I was someone she loved made me feel a tad uncomfortable. Love wasn't a word that was used in my house, and I rarely, if ever, heard it.

Fulton's eyes glided over my ankles, reminding me that my ankles were now in casts, and he asked, "How are you feeling?"

I willed my brain to focus on my feet, but no pain came. "I think I'm still numb."

"That's good." He added a reassuring nod.

"I wonder how long that should last." I thought out loud as I was used to ankle pain. I was used to a lot of body pain from dance, but the anticipation of wondering how bad it was going to be once I finally did feel it tugged at my nerves.

Fulton must have read my apprehension because he said, "It will be alright. Millie and I will take care of you." At that, we both looked back at Millie, who was hypnotized by her show.

A chuckle slipped out of my lips. "If she's going to take care of me, I'm in trouble."

"Don't worry. I can handle her if she gets out of hand."

A nurse came into the room carrying a water pitcher, and walked in front of Fulton, before greeting me, "Oh, good, you're awake. How are you feeling?"

"I'm okay." I shrugged, still unsure of what I should be feeling. "A little groggy."

"That's good to hear." She reached over to my beside table and filled my cup with fresh water and set the pitcher next to my cup before squaring her gaze with mine. "I'm Amy, and I'll be taking care of you while you're here."

"Thank you." My response came out more like a question, which surprised me, but I reasoned it had to be from this knot in my throat.

"So, after every surgery we do," she went on, "we want to make sure your bowels are moving again, so let me know if you pass some gas."

My cheeks heated at the mention of my bowels in front of Fulton. It was moments like these that made me resent my mom's lack of involvement. A girl needs her mother *sometimes*.

Amy continued to speak, "Other than that, things are going according to plan. Did you have any questions?"

I risked looking up. "How long do you think it will be before I can go?"

"I can't say for sure. Everyone's body reacts differently, but my guess is that it won't be long." She slid a thermometer across my forehead and waited for it to give a reading before she said, "These things can't be rushed."

"I understand.

She wrote down my temperature and then looked back at me. "You can eat now. I encourage you to do so, because it will speed up your bowels. If you must go to the bathroom, give me a call. In the meantime, is there anything else you can think of that you need?" She pulled her stethoscope up and plugged the buds into her ears.

I waited until she was done listening to my heart, and then asked, "Do you have anything with internet access?"

"You can use your cell phones." She gestured forward casually. "It used to be a hospital policy you couldn't use them, but they changed it."

I hesitated for a moment while I debated if I should be truthful, but then eventually decided it can't hurt. "We don't have phones."

"You don't have phones?" She peered at me over her clipboard as if she had heard incorrectly.

"No," I continue to speak softly because I understood how crazy this was to hear. "Our parents are making us participate in a weird social experience they call 'living off-grid' and we had to give up all that stuff."

She tilted her head and gave me a suspicious side eye. "For real?"

"Yes, unfortunately for us, it's for real."

"When's the last time you used the internet?"

I looked at Fulton, who shrugged his shoulders. Then I replied for us both, "About five weeks."

Her eyes widened in surprise. "That's crazy. Tell you what I can do: I'll bring in my personal laptop. I have it here because I edit photos on my break, but you can use it until then."

"Really?" I did my best to tone down my excitement, but inside my stomach was whooshing with anticipation. "Thank you so much!"

"Give me a few minutes to make my rounds down this way, and then I'll bring it in." She gathered her supplies and left the room. I couldn't avoid looking at Fulton, who was smirking at me. "Jackpot!" I joked.

"Sneaking the internet." He shook his head at me like I had done something terribly wrong, but I could tell by how wide his eyes were that he was just as excited as I was.

I sarcastically shook my head. "Might as well call juvie on me."

"I should but I don't have a phone."

I let out a fake laugh. "I feel like such a loser trying to explain to people why I don't have internet."

"It's hard to explain our ridiculous life."

"It is ridiculous, isn't it?" I stared into space to remember everything that we had been through recently. Sitting in the hospital bed, away from the farm and without my parents, gave me a little more clarity to what my life looked like from the outside. It was one of those things that if you didn't learn to laugh about it, you'd probably end up crying. Although I did cry my share of tears, I might have finally been able to see the humor in it. At least until I had to go back.

"Totally ridiculous," Fulton agreed. Then he shuffled some bags near his feet until he found the one he was looking for and held it out to me. "Before I forget, Millie and I got you a present."

"I want to give it to her!" Millie interrupted so loudly it startled me. She had been so quiet, I had forgotten she was still in the room. She jumped up and yanked the bag from Fulton, who was wide-eyed by her sudden springing to life. "Here, this is your present." She eagerly dropped the bag in my lap.

I looked at the gift-store bag and immediately felt emotional. "You guys . . . you didn't have to get me anything." I peeked in the bag and pulled out a fluffy, white blanket. "You got me a blanket?"

"Millie wanted to get you flowers, but I hate buying flowers because they die right away. So, we went to the gift shop instead, and I saw this blanket. Millie said it felt like a warm hug. I don't know, I guess it might be dumb, but I feel sort of bad your dad couldn't come, and you're stuck with us so . . . if you don't like it, you can take it back."

I rubbed my fingers along the corner, smoothing down the shaggy faux fur. "I love it," I blurted out. My eyes met Fulton's for the briefest of moments. "Thank you."

"You're welcome," Fulton said with a half-smile that grabbed my attention. I knew all his smiles, but I've never seen this one before, and I could see right through it. It was staged for me to conceal his concern. I lingered on it for a moment before Millie grabbed the blanket from me.

"I'll help you put it on so it fits like a hug," she instructed as she proceeded to wrap it around my shoulders. "Soft and cozy, like a hug," she added when she stood back and admired how she had wrapped me.

I squeezed my shoulders together, savoring the softness. "This is cozy."

"Look, I can even share it with you." Millie dropped down to sit next to me again and crawled inside it, smushing her tiny frame next to me. "Now this is really cozy."

"Yeah, it is," I agreed, feeling like a mama bird with a baby bird tucked under my wing. "Thank you both so much." I intentionally looked at each of them again, as a sting started to form in the backs of my eyes.

"Glad you like it," Fulton said as he held my eye contact while still wearing his fake smile.

"No, I mean it." My voice cracked out of nowhere and that triggered the tears to sting even harder, but I pushed through it. "Thanks for everything. For being here today. You guys rock."

"Don't mention it." Fulton waved his hand in the air, physically dismissing my comment. "We enjoyed it."

The fact that he was happy to be here made me chew my lip, my thoughts racing. Maybe it was the meds still wearing off, because I'm never this open with anyone but I spoke honestly, "I think if the tables were turned, I don't think I would have done this for you."

Fulton eyes bounced from mine to Millie, who smiled at him like she was a proud mama, and then he leveled his gaze back with mine. "I know you wouldn't have. But this is the kind of thing we do."

Now I know these meds messed me up or maybe it was the loneliness from my parents not being there, but I felt so bad for how I had treated him. During all the years back in New York, I was a total snob to him. The guilt knotted in my stomach, and I blurted out, "I can't understand why you would do this for me," I finally said.

"It's just a gift." He gave me a dismissing smile, but then he added, "I know this has to be hard for you having us here. I'm sorry your mom couldn't come."

It was like the word mom was a trigger to break the dam holding back my tears. I turned my head to avoid looking at them. Millie put her head down on my shoulder. "It's okay, Abs. We love you."

I tried to talk, but my words were silent. I mouthed, "I know," back to Millie.

My house windows were already darkened for the night by the time we arrived home. Annoyance flooded my veins when I realized neither one of my parents stayed awake to help me. Fulton parked the truck next to the front step. "I'll grab your dad." Just as he was about to go into my house, we saw Eddie and Linda run out from across the yard. "What's up?" Fulton asked them.

Linda opened the passenger door, and her voice came out frantic, "Let me talk to Abs." She took a step back when she saw Millie had fallen asleep on my shoulder, and she motioned to Eddie, who walked over, picked Millie up, and headed back inside their home with her. I was confused when Linda leaned in. "How are you doing?"

Her face was a shade paler than what was normal for her and paired it with my darkened house, I knew something was wrong. "What's going on?"

"I don't know how to say this, and I'm sorry it happened now." Her face pinched where her usual smile lines had straightened, making her look scared.

I already knew.

I couldn't wait for her to say it, and I stiffened, bracing myself to numb my emotions. "It's my mom, right?"

She nodded, bouncing her head several times. "She got sick, and your dad had to take her in."

"So that's where they are?" I tried to sound cool, like it didn't bother me, but I felt the sting of resentment boil in my chest. *Or maybe it was fear.*

"He took our truck since you had his, so we had no way of letting you know. I feel awful." Her forehead lines stacked all the way to her hairline, but she didn't break eye contact has she poured her heart out, "This night has done my heart in. I'm getting us all cell phones first thing in the morning. Off-grid living's great, but there's nothing wrong with having a phone for emergencies."

"So, no one's home?" I asked while glaring back at the dark house. The house I still hated, and it still didn't feel like home.

She shook her head, but rushed to smooth things over, "Your dad feels awful. You don't have to worry, though. I got you taken care of."

"How's that going to work?" My voice cracked as I realized how totally screwed I was going to be. "I'm not supposed to put weight on my ankles for weeks."

"Your dad will be back when he can, but I went ahead and washed your parents' bedding so you can sleep downstairs for now. I'll sleep at your house on the sofa, and I'll be right here if you need anything." Her voice was so reassuring. She made me want to believe everything was going to be okay even though inside my chest was getting tighter. This is the one time I needed my mom for real, and once again she failed to even be home.

Linda reached over taking my hand into her, before tossing a look over her shoulder and waved over at Fulton. "Can you help Abs into the house? Let's make her comfortable. She's probably exhausted." I was frozen as I watched her, and Fulton exchange a look. His obedience to her pulled at my heart. Man, I wanted that kind of relationship with my mom—or even my dad.

Heck, anybody would do at this point.

That's the look that emboldened into my brain with so much jealousy. I went through the motions of getting out of the truck, but I was fully inside my head wishing that someday, I would have someone look at me like that too.

Chapter Eleven

The next morning, my dad's face, shadowed with new facial hair, peeked through the bedroom door. "You up?"

I pulled myself up to sit and immediately winced from the pain radiating from my ankle. "I just woke up."

"How are you feeling?" His words were timid, like they were easing into ice water.

"Everything hurts. My ankles hurt, but I'm also sore from lying down."

"I read the discharge papers you had laying out there. They said it'll take a while before you won't need pain medication. You're only on day one."

"I know." My eyes landed on the skin puffed up under his eyes. He had aged a noticeable amount in the short time we had been in Montana. His skin was cracked by his eyes and even his lips looked dried. But it was more than just physical. He lacked the usual energetic charisma he always had in New York. It made me wonder if living here was everything he had wanted it to be, or perhaps he had regrets.

"I'm sorry I couldn't be there." His tone was too casual for an apology. I refused to let him off the hook so easily as I stayed silent until he added, "Did Linda explain what happened?"

I stubbornly looked past his head out the door. "Not really."

After a long pause, he said, "I think you've been through enough."

My heart gave first, pounding hard against my chest, and it forced my eyes to cave to search for his, ready to hear whatever it was. "Is it the same as last time?"

He offered a slow shrug, and for a moment I felt like I've seen this scene before. This whole speech. Everything about it. "Her doctor said it was a nervous breakdown."

"Is she okay?" My words floated out, which surprised me that I even asked because I don't think I would have been able to hear the answer if she hadn't been.

"They moved her to the psych ward this morning. I wanted to stay with her, but you know how she is when she's there. It's better to let her simmer. Plus, I knew you were here. It's an impossible situation . . ." His voice trailed off and he slowly made his way to the bed and sat down.

"I'm fine." I put my hand on his back. It was a knee-jerk response that had me screaming inside how messed up this was. "You can go be with her. You don't have to worry about me. It's not like I can go anywhere anyway." I forced a smile, knowing that he needed it, but it killed me to do it. All I wanted was for him to comfort me, but instead I was the one comforting him.

"I knew you would be my strong girl." His eyes told me that his words were true, but I hated them. When I didn't reply, he added, "Did everything go alright?"

"I think so. I have a checkup in a couple weeks." I blinked away my immediate frustration that my dad didn't know how my surgery went.

"Good, that should give me time to get your mom settled into an aftercare program."

I furrowed my eyebrows for so many reasons. First, I was upset that we were already talking about her again when he only gave me one whole sentence to talk about what I went through, but mostly because she'd never done an aftercare program before. "She doesn't get to come back here?"

"I would be more comfortable if she were in an in-patient program this time. That way she has around-the-clock care. Besides, she doesn't act like she wants to be here."

I narrowed my eyes in concentration, as nothing about that seemed fair. "I don't want to be here either, but I still came back."

My dad reached up to rub the facial hair on his chin, but it didn't seem to calm him as the lines in his forehead deepened, and his voice dropped, "Not here on the farm. Here in general." The look on his face made me hurt for him. My hand was still resting on his back, and I pulled the other one around him and squeezed. I didn't want to know what had happened. I didn't need that visual. I leaned my forehead on his arm, and my eyes fell, landing on my blanket. I recalled how Fulton had given it to me because he thought I needed a hug from my dad. It was sadly ironic that even now with my dad sitting next to me, I was the one hugging him.

Someday, I told myself, I wouldn't have to be the strong one.

Later that morning, my dad had left, and I was alone again when Linda carried a tray into my room. The dishes made soft clanging noises as they barely bumped together as she walked, but the sound instantly awakened my appetite. "I brought you some homemade goat's milk yogurt with choke cherry syrup and eggs."

"That smells amazing." My stomach rumbled in agreement.

"I saw that your dad was home." She carefully set the tray over my lap. Then she took an extra moment to smooth the bedspread around me. "By the way, we don't have any fresh water while that pipe's still broken, so try not to waste what we have stored."

I flicked a finger out to point at my casts. "You don't have to worry about me."

The smile she gave me was gentle, almost as if she was testing my response. "Are you doing better today?"

I nodded because it was the only way I could lie to her. I didn't need her to know how my chest felt so tight that sometimes I have to place my hand on top of it to make sure I was still breathing.

She took a step closer and lowered herself onto the bed to sit next to me. "I sent Eddie to town to get us phones. I can't have a night like last night again. My heart can't do it. Did your dad tell you about it?"

"Sort of." I kept my gaze down and poked at my eggs with my fork, not wanting to get into this conversation with Linda. Or with anyone.

"Well, she's going to be fine. Don't worry about her. You need to focus on you right now."

"Easier said than done." I took a small bite of eggs and chewed, letting the peppery sting absorb into my tongue.

"Keep your mind on happy things."

"It's pretty hard to find a distraction when you live off-grid in a tiny home and can't use your legs."

Her eyes held a tinge of excitement, but just like the smile Fulton had given me yesterday, I knew it was forced. "Oh, that reminds me. I have something to occupy some of your time with!"

"What?" I asked not unkindly. Part of my chest filled with hope. *Please be a TV.* Even though there was a strict no-technology rule, they had to know it was better for my brain to watch TV than just stare at the ceiling all day.

"Millie fell in love with your pants. She wants you to put a patch on her pants too. She wants a unicorn."

I let that sink in. It wasn't at all what I expected. Frankly it was too much work. "Can't you just do it? You're the sewer."

"I could, but I would rather we do it together. That way we get to hang out."

I resisted the sigh begging to leak out. "You're trying to find a reason to babysit me."

"No, not at all. You don't need me to watch you. Sewing could be good for you. Maybe not forever, but at least while you can't use your legs. What else are you going to do?"

Well, since you asked, I was hoping for a TV. My inner voice did nothing to make me feel better. "You have a point.

"Is that a yes?" She leaned forward slightly while she waited on my answer, as if the excitement was so strong she couldn't sit still.

"I guess," I said with an exhalation. Not because I wanted to do it. I might still be a little bitter about the TV. This was for Linda. I didn't want to disappoint her.

"This is going to be so fun." The warm smile she had on her face grew wider. "I'll run back and grab my sewing basket. We might as well get started now."

Since I was done eating, she grabbed my tray. With her free hand she smoothed out my blanket, tidying up my bed. "I'll put these in the kitchen, and I'll be right back. Don't go anywhere." She chuckled at her joke, but I couldn't even force a smile.

"Like that's going to be hard."

She tossed a quick look back over her shoulder when she got to the doorway. "Is there anything else I can grab for you?"

"No, thank you." I paused and then I surprised myself by saying, "It's not the first time." My words echoed in the room as I stared at her, not wanting her to leave me alone. I hadn't planned on talking. I never talked about it, but her gestures were so kind they had a way of opening me up.

"I know." It ripped at my heart the way her eyes locked on mine, like she was truly dialed in. My mom had never looked at me like that.

"You do?" I blinked back a budding tear, hating that my mom had this effect on me, when it's so obvious that she didn't care about me.

She gave me one of those non-committal nods like she wasn't sure where this conversation was going, but she didn't want to speak because she knew it would interrupt my willingness to talk.

"What do you know?" I clenched the edge of my blanket as it had quickly become my security object.

She set the tray on the edge of my bed and sat back down, closer to me this time. She lightly touched my hand, and I suddenly felt super exposed. It was like her touch opened my protective shield. "I know that when you say it's happened before, you don't mean it happened *only once* before."

I held my gaze steady on her, and my voice cracked when I asked, "You do?"

"I know." She added a second non-committal nod, which had me a little in awe of how good she was staying neutral. Not a single ounce of judgement flowed out of her. All I felt was pure support.

"Do you know about my birthdays she missed?" My bottom lip quivered, and I rolled it in to hide it.

She nodded her head again all the while her gaze never left me, and she stayed silent and ready to listen.

"Do you know that she's never seen me dance in a recital?" I'm not sure where that question even came from. It spewed out like it was sitting at the top of my chest for years.

Another perfect nod with so much direct eye contact. I don't think I've ever felt this seen before.

"Not even the time I got to be the principal ballerina." My voice pitched higher with this statement as if I'm on a mission to expose my mom for all the things she never did.

Linda's tone was even, soothing, "I know."

"Do you know what it means to be the principal ballerina? It's the rarest honor. Like, it almost never happens, and it happened to me." I was rambling, trying to get everything out before I lost my courage. "I danced four hours a day to get that role. I woke up and danced before school, I danced on my lunch break, I danced after school. I danced so hard it put me in these stupid casts!" I yelled the last part. My heart slammed against my chest wall, and I struggled to breath, but I barreled on, "Do you know why I danced so hard?" I didn't wait for her to answer me. I sat up taller, as best as I could do for being post-surgery and gave her a pointed glare. "I wanted her to care. To notice. To say she was proud of me." A single tear streamed down my face, but my mom didn't deserve that. I swiped it away with the back of my hand. "All my friends were there, my teachers were there, the reporter from the newspaper was there—they took my picture and put it in the paper and said how great I was. They all said I was great. They all came. But do you know who didn't come? She didn't come. She got sick. I made her sick!" I dropped my face into my hands, and now the fountain of tears I'd been holding onto for years, unleashed and I just wept.

Linda wrapped her arms around me, bringing her warmth right to me and held me as I sobbed. "You didn't cause it."

"I did." I buried my head in Linda's shoulder, taking in her sweet, motherly scent, which only made me cry harder because I've never had this experience of being held by a mother—any mother—while I cried.

"No, you didn't. Don't think that. You didn't do it, and she didn't make it happen either. It just happened." She continued to hold me tightly, and the feeling of constriction helped to keep me from screaming what was inside my head.

"Every time I need her, she gets sick," my voice was so tiny as I squeezed my words out through sobs. "I just had surgery; I needed her, and she got sick. Why do I cause it?"

"You don't, honey," she said softly. "I don't have an answer, but I do know you didn't do it. I know it's incredibly painful, but she can't help it. She has a tough time with things."

"But so do I! Why can't I ever be the broken one?"

"You don't have to be strong all the time." She pulled out of our hug, but quickly locked her gaze on me, and slowly started to rub my back. "You're allowed to be broken too."

"I don't get it. I thought coming here was supposed to fix her. She destroyed my life because she wanted this, and it still isn't enough." I reached for my hug blanket, and I pulled it against my stomach.

"I'm not sure if she knew what she wanted. I think she had a lot of excuses, like she didn't like her job, she didn't like the commute, she didn't like the craziness of city life. I think she told herself that if she could get rid of those things, she would be better. But after she got rid of them, she was left with no excuses. That was scary for her. She had to see what she was really disliking, and she found it in herself."

My jaw dropped open as I hadn't thought of it like that, but it made so much sense. "She told you that?"

"In ways she has. I have known her for a long time. Some stuff I have watched her go through. Other stuff I have heard about. I'm sure there is more I don't know." She grabbed my hand and squeezed. "I know she loves you."

"You can't know that. My mom doesn't know how to love. And neither do I."

Chapter Twelve

I woke up every day eager for my ankles to feel better, but the time they were taking to heal made my patience frail, especially since Linda constantly hovered over me, encouraging me to sew decorative patches on every piece of fabric she could find. It was sweet relief when I finally got permission to leave the house for my checkup. As I was leaving, my dad handed me two fifty-dollar bills. "Here's the money for lunch and gas. You kids did a good job last time, so I'm trusting you again."

"I'll be fine. I got my emergency cell phone this time if anything happens." I pointed to my purse right as Millie came running out of the house and crawled over top of me to get to the middle seat on the pickup bench.

"Let me help," my dad said, and he lifted her until she was able to find her footing. "Watch out that you don't kick Ab's casts. We want a good doctor's report."

Fulton jogged over to the truck. He was wearing faded jeans and a white T-shirt. His previously buzzed hair had grown a lot since we arrived on the farm, and this morning he combed it back out of his face, leaving only a couple of wispy strands of hair to fall by his eyes. I did a double take as I had gotten used to seeing him in his work coveralls. It's like he dressed up for something. "Sorry you guys had to wait," Fulton's words puffed out as he was out of breath. "My mom was giving me all the rules."

"How can anyone add anymore rules to the ones we already have," I half joked.

"Oh, she had a few." He chuckled and ran around to his side of the truck and got in. As soon as Fulton was seated, I looked back at my dad. "I think we're ready to leave."

Dad's gaze shifted to Fulton and then back to me. "Are you sure you don't want me to come with?"

I didn't care either way, but Fulton was acting weird about this trip to town. He begged my dad to let him take me again, citing a need for fast food and the internet. Now that he was all dressed up, I'm even more curious as to what's going on. I looked at Fulton, who was giving me a please-don't-blow-this look. Whatever he was up to, I wanted to find out, so I turned back to my dad and said, "We'll be fine."

"Alright, honey, be careful." He closed the door for me and took a step back, planting his feet on the ground, intent on watching us drive away.

I waved goodbye as Fulton pulled the truck forward. After we were around the bend and heading out to the highway, I turned to him with an inquiring mind, "So what's up?"

"Why do you think something's up?" His eyes stayed locked on the road ahead of him, but I didn't miss the telling twitch in the corner of his lips.

"I know you don't love going to doctor's appointments, and you're all dressed up." I rolled my window down, letting the air whip my previously neat hair. I gathered it back into a ponytail. I didn't have a hairband with me so I spiraled it up on top of my head into a bun and used the ends to tangle it enough so it wouldn't fall out.

He glanced at me a couple of times, waiting for me to get done with my hair like he had this big speech he was going to give. "You're going to find out anyway."

"Find out what?" Now I was super curious how he had plans, because we were so cut off from society, there wasn't even a way to make plans. "Are you running away?"

"No." His chuckle lasted for only one beat before he swapped back to his serious face. "I have an appointment too. I don't want to say what it's for yet, but I'll drop you off at the clinic with Millie, and I'll come back to get you when I'm done."

"You're ditching a girl who can't walk?" I was more intrigued than I was annoyed, but I didn't want to let him off easy.

"You'll be okay." He stole another look at me before returning his eyes to the road. "I've thought this through. I'll help you get inside with the wheelchair, and Millie can help you from there. I'll come as soon as I'm done."

I grew a real smirk for the first time in a long time. "Fulton Rogers, how dare you have a life outside the homestead."

The lines on his forehead softened and he gave me a cheeky grin that only fueled my curiosity. "I know, right? How dare I do something for myself."

"So, what are you up to?" I studied his side profile for any clues of dishonesty.

"I'll tell when I can," his words came out fast, and then he pinched his lips together as if to physically seal in his secrets.

"Promise?"

He nodded, reassuringly. "Promise. You'll be the first to know."

When my checkup was complete, Fulton still hadn't shown up at the clinic to pick us up, so Millie wheeled me out to the curbside. I looked down the street, but there was no sign of him. "Just what is that brother of yours up to?"

"I don't know," Millie said from behind my chair. "It's starting to feel a little fishy."

"What's he been doing at home? Anything weird?"

"We've all been doing weird stuff."

"Good point." I chuckle. "I should ask if he has been doing anything normal."

"Yeah, that would be weird."

My gaze rose to the sky that was growing gray. "It looks like it's going to rain soon. We can go back inside and watch TV, or I think that's a coffee shop across the street. Do you want to wheel me there?"

"I'd rather wait here so Fulton can find us." Her lips pursed nervously as her eyes darted up and down the street.

"I think if we grab a table by the window, I'll be able to watch for him." I was a little worried too—Fulton was never tardy—but I took reassurance in the fact he did say he had an appointment.

She eyebrows raised as her tone perked up, "Can I get a Frappuccino?"

"Absolutely. It's my treat." I was happy to have a diversion to offer her.

Millie pushed me across the street, and once we were inside, Millie effortlessly glided my chair to a booth by the window. I scooted out of my chair and slid onto the bench. She tucked my chair in a corner.

A waitress came over and handed us menus. "Good morning, ladies. How are you?"

"We are good," I replied as I smiled at Millie over my menu.

"I saw you came from the clinic," she said casually. "What happened?"

"I had double ankle surgery, and I got my walking boots today. I'm not technically wheelchair-bound, but they want to start me off slowly with exercises before I start walking."

"It looks like you have a good helper." She nodded at Millie, who couldn't resist staring out the window as she already sat up on her knees with her face almost pressed to the glass.

"She's the best." I enjoyed the way Millie's face lit up from the compliments, even though she still had a worry line pinned between her eyebrows.

The waitress straightened her pen over her pad of paper. "Do you know what you ladies would like?"

Millie twisted on her knees, redirecting her focus to the woman. "Mocha Frappuccino, please."

"Do you want toppings?" the waitress asked.

Millie gave me a mischievous smile before she replied, "All of them."

"You got it, hon." She added a wink in Millies's direction. "I'll give you my version of diabetes in a cup."

Millie giggled like she was already being fed spoonfuls of artificially dyed sugar candies.

"I'm in trouble," I said with a laugh. "I better have strong black coffee so I can stay on top of my sugar-high chauffeur."

"That's probably a good choice." She grabbed our menus and then gestured toward my leg. "Cute jeans, by the way. Those patchy things you have are super cute. I saw hers and I thought maybe it was something the younger girls had." She motioned to Millie. "Then when you got out of your chair, I saw you had one too. Is that the in-thing now?"

"I doubt it." I resisted the urge to roll my eyes as the mere thought of these patches and all the sewing I did gave me an instant headache. "I actually made them because my parents are on a no-buying things kick."

"They are adorable." She smiled at each of us one more time, before taking a step back and saying, "I'll be right back with your drinks."

"There he is." Millie moved all the way over in the booth again and tapped the window. Finally, the worry line that was pinned between her brows fell. Even though I wouldn't admit I was a tad worried, I felt a breath of relief slip out of my lips. Fulton had parked the truck in the loading zone at the hospital and was rushing toward the entrance. "He doesn't know we're are here." She cut her gaze back to me. "Can I run over there?"

"You can, but please be careful crossing that street." At that, Millie ran out of the coffee shop, and I watched her scurry across the street. When Fulton saw her, they both hopped in his truck and drove it to the coffee shop. Our drinks came while I waited. I sat back in the booth, sipping my coffee, and noticed a gift section at the other end of the room. If I had legs that worked, I would have walked over there to shop. I could see coffee mugs, candles, and small items that mostly looked homemade and unattractive, but it had been forever since I'd indulged in retail therapy. I was itching for the release so badly I would have shopped a shelf of algebra books if that would have been available.

Finally, after a few minutes, Fulton sprinted through the door, pulling Millie behind him.

He slid into the booth to sit next to the window, leaving room for Millie. Millie's jaw dropped when she saw her drink heaped with whipped cream, sprinkles, chocolate chips, marshmallows, and chocolate syrup. "Yummy." She dipped her finger right in the middle of the toppings, collecting a huge sugary glop, and plopped it into her mouth. "That tastes amazing."

"I can see what you two have been up to while I was gone." Fulton tried to sneak Millie's straw for a taste, but she stopped him.

"It's all mine." With a devilish smile, she pulled it closer to her body, protecting it from Fulton's hands.

"Excuse me," Fulton said with a laugh, and then he turned away and gave her the privacy to gorge in peace. He looked at me, and paused for a beat as if waiting to see what kind of mood I was in. "I'm sorry for being late. Forgive me."

I looked at him slyly as I studied his expression for any clues of what he had been up to. Same clean clothes with no food stains or anything. His hair was still neat, which means he had to be inside and out of the wind. He wasn't giving me any clues, and I wasn't letting him off the hook. "Depends."

There was more amusement than annoyance in his expression. "On what?"

I took a dramatic sip of my coffee, while keeping my gaze locked with his, and after the longest pause, I said, "On what you were up to."

I was surprised he didn't immediately refuse. Instead, his gaze bounced to Millie. "Millie, can you let me talk to Abs for a second?"

"You want me to leave?" Her head tilted toward him as a look of bewilderment settled on her face.

"No. you don't have to leave." He inserted a sigh while he thought for a beat and then pointed to her head. "Can you plug your ears and look the other way?"

Her brows bent down, but her smile didn't deflate. "Are you serious?"

"Give me your head." Fulton reached over to cover her ears with his hands. She giggled like it was a game, but she trusted him and leaned over until he had both of her ears cupped. "Can you hear me?" he asked.

"What did you say?" She grinned, obviously enjoying the attention.

With a full smile I rarely see on his face, Fulton leaned forward and spoke in a hushed voice. "I talked to my friend, Brent, who I was going to live with this fall, back in New York."

I leaned forward, already completely invested. "Yeah . . . and?"

"His dad got fired for some embezzlement thing. They have to move out of state. So, I can't stay with him anymore."

"That stinks." My tone is neutral as I'm not really sure how I feel about it. I hadn't really pictured Fulton getting to leave.

His gaze lowered to Millie. When he was satisfied that she wasn't listening, he continued. "I've been trying to line up something else but it's not looking too good."

"You mean you won't be able to move back?" I tried to hide my relief. We aren't best friends, but it's not fair if he gets to go back, and I'm stuck on the farm with just Millie.

"No, I'm moving back as soon as I turn eighteen," he asserts. "I need to line up a place to stay. I thought about renting an apartment, but I'd have to get a roommate to afford it, and it's impossible to coordinate any of this stuff when I have no internet access, and our only phone is on lockdown in my mom's room."

"Are you guys talking about me?" Millie twisted sideways until Fulton removed his hands from her ears. "Yep, we were talking about you. I told her all about how you used to pee the bed."

Millie's mouth dropped. "You did not!"

"Well, *you* just did," I said with a serious tone.

Fulton let a relaxed grin rest on his face. "I can't win with you two."

"You're mean." Millie glared at her brother and folded her hands across her chest

"It's fine. We all did that," I reassured Millie. She stared at me, surprised. "Really," I affirmed. "Actually, I've been peeing in a bed pan for weeks now. How do you think that makes me feel?"

She wrinkled her nose. "That's gross."

"I know." I nodded, disgusted by my own life. The stranger thing is that I wasn't embarrassed admitting that to either of them. I could have never on any planet admitted that to Tina or Becky, but Millie and Fulton and I have somehow formed this weird little club, where we don't judge because we're all in the same boat.

Our waitress walked back up to the table and slid our ticket on the end of it. "Anything else you need before I leave this?"

I looked at Fulton, who never had a chance to order, but he shook his head, so I replied, "I don't think so."

"Well, before you leave, I was going to ask if you have a website. My granddaughter dances. She would love a pair of jeans like that."

I stared blankly at her for a second until I remembered her compliment about my jeans, and I let out a light chuckle. "No, I don't make them to sell. I only made a couple pairs."

"There you go, Abs," Fulton interjected. "You need a business anyway. You can patch people's jeans."

"No, it's not on my Bingo card." I shook my head but did my best to smile kindly at the lady.

She took a step back from the table, reached over the bar counter, and retrieved a card. Handing it to me, she said, "This is my card. If you ever decide you want to do another pair, I would love to buy one. This is actually my coffee shop. I'm always here. My name is Lynn."

I took her card, but only to be polite. There was no way I was going to make any more pairs of these pants. "Again, I appreciate your kind words, but it's not something I do for other people." I slid to the edge of the bench and readied myself to get up.

"I understand completely." She moved away from the table, and Millie helped me into my chair. We were silent until we were back in the truck.

Fulton started the truck but stared forward. After a few minutes, I nudged him. "What are you waiting for? Let's go."

His eyes were soft in an apologetic way when he turned to me. "I was going to ask if you wanted to stop to see your mom . . . you know, since we're in town, but I wasn't sure if I was allowed to bring it up."

My throat got instantly dry, and I didn't even know how to respond. Instead, I blanked out staring back at him.

"Forget I brought it up." He shifted the truck into gear and turned to pull out but stopped when I started talking.

"I just don't see what purpose it would serve." My chest tightened, as I felt like I needed to defend my lack of excitement. "When I was little, I used to want to go see her. I needed to tell her what I had been up to, and all the things she was missing, because I had believed she actually cared."

"She does care." Fulton gave me a side-eye.

"I honestly don't know if she does or not, but she's not usually herself." I rolled my eyes to no one. It felt good to have some sort of physical release. "They put her on all sorts of medication. Most of the time she doesn't remember if I came or not."

"I didn't know it was like that." His gaze bounced all around my face as if he was waiting for me to expound, but I've never spoken about any of this to anyone, and I said enough.

The silence drug on as Fulton held space for me. I get we were in this weird friendship stage now, and I oddly trusted him, but that didn't mean I was going to willingly give up all my secrets.

After the longest pause, Millie huffed out, "Can we get going?"

Fulton looked over at her perched in between us. "What are you in such a hurry for?"

"Remember? Dad's bringing my pony home today."

"Oh man, I forgot." Fulton mocked disappointment but pulled the truck forward and then added in an exaggerated voice, "Emergency, it's pony day!"

"I didn't know you were getting a horse." My statement came out sounding more like a question.

"She is," Fulton said. "The neighbor to the south of us had one that he was getting tired of feeding, She's old, and she doesn't do much except eat and sleep. He's letting us have her. She's slow and you can't ride her, but she's good with kids."

"I'm going to call her Sundance," Millie stated.

"I remember you telling me at dinner, back in New York, that you liked that name," I said. "What makes that name so special?"

Her lips turned up like she was keeping a secret. "Come on, I don't have to tell you about dancing."

My brow bent down as I somehow missed the punchline. I was confused by her assuming I knew what was going on. "What do you mean?"

"You know, dancing's like a special way to go through life where you don't stop for any of the bad things."

I looked at Fulton and twisted my thumb toward her. "Is she only eight years old?"

"Sounds to me like she's a twenty-five-year-old philosophy major."

"How did you come up with that?" I stared at her with amusement.

"You guys." She smacked her palm on her forehead. "Do I have to teach you everything?"

Fulton took a sharp right, and I swayed leaning on Millie, and I wrapped my arm around her shoulders to prevent squishing her. It felt natural to do that, but inside I was thinking that she was easily the best part of this move. My thoughts were interrupted by the sound of rain splattering on the windshield. Fulton turned the windshield wipers on, but they were squeaking as they tried to keep up.

Fulton accelerated the truck, and spoke as if he was thinking out loud, "We need to get back before the dirt road gets too muddy and slick."

The squeak of the wipers only got worse, and they barely did anything to clear the window. "I need to tell dad he needs new wipers—"

"Hold on!" Fulton screamed and tried to serve but it was too late because the truck jerked to a stop when we heard a thunk.

My mouth dropped as I stared at Fulton." What did you just hit?"

Chapter Thirteen

"It's a dog," Fulton called through the pounding rain from his spot near the front bumper. "He's still alive."

Millie instantly burst into tears. "We can't leave him here!"

"Don't worry, Millie, we won't," I said. Then I stuck my head out the window and yelled to Fulton, "Bring him inside the truck and we can look for the owner tomorrow after the rain stops."

Fulton came around my side of the truck, cradling the soaking canine.

I pushed my door open and what I saw made me wince in empathy. His leg was bent in an unnatural way. I did my best to take the dog carefully, but he cried, and he was too heavy to move with ease. Fulton ran back around the truck and got in his seat. I tried to sit as still as I could when I pulled out my phone in search of a veterinarian to call. I scrolled through the lists of numbers, hitting call on the one closest to our location. "They're closing," I reported after ending the call, "but the receptionist saidthey would wait for us if we leave right now."

"This is going to take too long to bring you guys with." He took the phone from my hands. "I'm calling my dad to pick you up. It'll only take two extra minutes." I stayed silent because I knew he didn't want to mess with me and Millie on top of the dog. I agreed and waited for help to arrive.

Later that night, I flipped my pillow for the zillionth time, trying to find a cool spot to rest my face on. The wind howled above my head. Frustrated by my lack of sleep, I gave up and sat up to check the storm. The rain had ceased but it was the wind's turn to solo dance. The clouds had cloaked the moon, blackening the already dark night. I leaned on my window ledge, resting my chin on my arm, both mesmerized and freaked out by the storm's intensity. A storm in the city is one thing. Out here in the middle of nowhere, I felt completely exposed.

A movement captured my attention. Fulton had stepped out of his home, carrying a bundle that I suspected was the dog we rescued. He darted to the shed and disappeared inside. I waited for his return, but after several long minutes, my curiosity got the best of me.

I wrapped myself in my hug blanket and eased out of bed. I clung to the wall as I wove my way outside. I inhaled the newly cleansed night air and braced myself for the wind's power as I waddled to the outbuilding.

"Should you be walking out here?" Fulton smirked when I approached. "You look like the mechanical creature from the portal of darkness with the way you are waddling."

"Haha." I stood in the doorway, peeking in. The shed had been emptied out except for some grain bins stored for animal feed, but those were pushed against the back wall. Fulton sat cross-legged on the wooden floor with the dog resting his chin on Fulton's leg. "So, what are you doing out here?"

Fulton nodded toward the dog. "She was crying, and I didn't want her to wake everyone up. I didn't know where else to go. You sort of run out of hiding places when you live in a tiny house."

"She's a girl?" I knelt next to the dog, slowly extending my upright palm out and under her nose. "How is she?"

"The vet said she broke two legs but didn't need any surgeries. He set her legs back into place and wrapped them." Fulton pointed to her back paws wrapped with skinny dog casts.

"I bet that stunk to watch her go through that," I kept my voice low, and the dog and I stared at each other, taking one another in.

"Actually, it was sort of interesting. I've never seen anything like it. The vet went right into action. I tried to comfort her, but she didn't seem to like me that much. She probably saw I was the one driving the pickup."

I let the dog lick my fingertips and smiled at the way her velvety tongue tickled. "Nah, she knows you're the one who rescued her."

"I'm not sure about that, but we did get some meds to help calm her down and for her pain." He pointed to my boots. "But the real question is: why are you out here in the middle of the storm? Or is bad weather what makes you transform and head back to your planet?"

"My planet?" I snorted, only half getting his joke. "Yep, headed back to my moon galaxy."

"Moon galaxy? That's not even a realistic exaggeration." He raised an eyebrow at me. "I was thinking something simple like Mars."

"Sorry, I wasn't a science genus like you. I'm lucky if I remember the name of this planet." I lowered my eyes, remembering how much I had hated going to school. Now the thought of it tugged at a place in my memories that only made me feel nostalgic for my other life. I didn't want to get sad, so I kept the focus on the dog. "I got nosey when I saw you out here. I had no idea you had a secretive nightlife too."

The dog whimpered. Fulton responded by stroking the fur along her back, which seemed to have a calming effect. He looked back at me and his eyes held a cautious layer. "About that . . ."

"What?"

"I have a favor to ask you."

"Now what?" I sat upright, trying to see his face better in the dark shed.

"I think I may have come up with a plan that'll work for me to get back to the city, but I need one more day in town to do some research on the internet."

"What does that have to do with me?"

"My parents aren't going to let me go into town to use the internet. They want me to be unplugged from all that."

"Why don't you just tell them why you need it?"

"If I tell them now, they'll probably feel hurt. Since I don't have anything organized yet, it will seem like I'm venting. I want to have all my plans in place so when I do tell them, they'll know I'm serious, and that I've thought everything out. I want them to know it's not to hurt their feelings, but it's what's right for me."

"Sorry, but I don't have any doctor appointments for a couple weeks." I wagged my head, not seeing anything I could do to help.

He gave me a pleading look. "But you do have something that could work."

"What's that?" I raised an eyebrow as adrenaline started to pump in my chest.

"That lady asked you to design some jeans for her granddaughter. You could tell your dad about her and say you thought about it, and you want to do it. Your dad will instantly be convinced it's a great idea, and we'll need to go into town to get supplies."

"But I don't like sewing. I'm only doing it to be nice to your mom because she's been so sweet to me."

"I know, but it's only one pair. And if you tell my mom about it, she'll help you."

Biting my lip, I think it over for a moment. It's not really that big of a deal. I guess. "So, you need me to tell my dad I have to go to town tomorrow?"

His eyes burned with urgency. "I would do it for you."

He didn't need to say it, because I knew he would do exactly that for me. This was the kind of friend he was, and the kind of friend I was slowly working towards. Even though I wasn't excited, I tugged the side of my lips into a lopsided grin. "I'll try first thing in the morning."

"Awesome." A sigh of relief dropped from his lips before he tacked on, "I'll owe you."

I pointed to the dog, whose eyelids were beginning to waver. "Do you know what kind of dog she is?"

"The vet said maybe some sort of Terrier cross. He thought maybe a mix with a lab or something taller, because she's big for a Terrier."

I tilted my head closer to the dog to study her. The only clue to her age were a few gray hairs dotting her snout. "What do you know about terriers?"

"Just what the vet said." He added a one shoulder shrug. "They can be very protective, especially of their owners—almost to the point of territorial. The vet didn't find a microchip either, so I guess we're adopting her unless someone comes forward, which will probably never happen. The vet said that a lot of people abandon unwanted dogs in the country. He thought that's probably what had happened."

"That's sad." I made a pouty face toward the dog because I understood her pain of having two broken legs and parents who didn't care about her.

"Millie named her Raindance since we found her in the rain."

My eyes rose back to meet his. "What's up with her and dance all of the sudden?"

"It's not really all that sudden." He shakes his head, completely dismissing my statement. "She's looked up to you for a long time."

"Me?" I wrinkled my nose. "I don't think it has anything to do with me."

"I think you're wrong. I remember last year when we went to see you dance at your recital. I looked at her while she was on the edge of her seat and was visually glued to you. She talked about it for months. Actually, she still brings it up."

"I didn't know she liked dance. She should've taken a class."

"I don't think she wants to dance. It's more like going to Disney World. She still lives in a world where she wants to believe in princesses and Santa Claus. You were dancing the part of a fairy, and she bought into it."

"I had no idea."

"You have that effect on people when you dance."

I bent my shoulders into a cringe. The old me would have expected a compliment about my dancing, but that seemed so long ago. "I didn't do anything any other ballerina wouldn't have done."

"It's your focus. I don't know anything about dance, but I can see you're intense in the most graceful way. You suck people right into your story."

"Wow, that's a really nice thing to say." I wasn't sure why Fulton felt the need to compliment me. In an odd way, it put a tiny patch on part of the gaping hole in my heart that was left from having to give everything up.

"I'm not telling you anything you didn't know. Everyone knew it. Even an eight-year-old like Millie."

"But I was so stuck-up and mean." I turned my face down, as if the mere action would hold back my memories.

"Millie didn't see any of that. She only saw what she wanted to see."

"Millie's a sweet little girl." A rush of shrill wind pushed into the shed. I wrapped my blanket tighter around my shoulders. "Somedays when we're hanging out together, it feels like she's my little sister. I think about what it would be like to have another person to grow up with."

"Do you think you've missed out on having a sibling?" His expression was so nonjudgemental, it made me want to be honest. I had no clue what had happened between the two of us lately. Somehow, we became friends. He always seemed to be the only one around for me to talk to, and he actually acted like he cared.

I let out a small sigh, as I dug deep for my true thoughts. "Nah, I wouldn't want to put another kid through having my mom."

Fulton continued to stroke Raindance's back. His silence wasn't one of lack of empathy, though. He understood. In a weird way, he was the one who knew my situation best, even better than Becky or Tina. Maybe even better than my dad.

"I do love Millie's definition of dance, though," I added, hoping to get the conversation back to a happier place

"Millie's intuitive. She knows what dance is to you." He shifted and leaned forward, aligning his face with the opened door that allowed a sliver of the Rogers' porch light to lighten the shadows on his face. Even though I see him every day, it was a rare moment where I really looked at him. The summer had treated him to a deep tan. His previously boney shoulders had broadened from working outside all summer. He looked much older than when we came to the farm. There was also something different about his demeanor too. I could tell that although the move had made my heart harder, it had softened his. He had always had a kind spirit, but being here had opened him up. I could see how he relaxed and gave up some of his previous nervous habits. I smiled when I realized the way I saw him had also changed. I no longer thought of him as a geek from school, but he was my close friend.

I took a deep breath, savoring the crisp smell of rain. "It's exactly what dance is to me. A way to keep moving time forward until the bad is in the past."

A loud popping sound suddenly came from behind the shed. "What do you think that was?" I asked, my shoulders stiff, afraid to look.

"Sounds like a branch probably cracked from the wind," Fulton thought out loud but made no effort to inspect it.

I looked nervously back outside and saw the wind had picked up. The shelter trees behind Fulton's house were bending and swaying so much, they looked ready to snap. "We should go inside," I suggested.

"You should." He nodded his head towards the direction of my house. "I'm going to stay with Raindance until she feels better. It's my fault she's hurt."

"It was an accident."

Fulton's eyes stayed steady on the dog, and I knew he was content. I stood, taking a step out, but stopped when I looked through the door. I'm usually sleeping at this hour, and I'd never seen some place so black. With the clouds covering the moon, it was if the whole world had gone dark. "It's so dark and creepy right now. There's literally no stars or moon."

"You need the moon to go back to your weird moon galaxy?" he teased.

"Hey, it's not any weirder than this place."

He chuckled. "I can only imagine. That'll be next spring. Our parents will come home and say we're building a spaceship and have to live on a new planet."

I put my hand up to stop him. "Don't even say it. They might hear you and get an idea."

"Yep, then instead of picking berries and milking cows, we'll be fighting aliens."

"You're funny."

"Not really. Totally serious."

"Stop it. I'm going to get creeped out talking about aliens out here."

"Nah, no need to get scared."

"Do you ever think about that stuff?" I searched the sky that was still so black.

"Aliens? No, because they're fake. I watched an internet video one time from an exorcist. He said that if God allowed all the angels and demons of the night to be seen, you wouldn't be able to see the moon, ever. They are so densely populated—both the good and the bad angels. That's the sort of stuff that weirds me out."

Goosebumps dotted my spine. "You believe in bad angels?"

He was thoughtfully quiet and then nodded. "I do."

"Do you believe in good angels? Like real ones with wings?"

"I think if you believe in one, you have to believe in the other. It's the dichotomy. You can't really have evil unless you have good, or it would all be the same. Do you know what I mean?"

"Not really. Or maybe a little."

"Do you believe in angels?"

I thought about my life and my mom and everything we'd all been through because of her condition. I'd heard people talk about guardian angels before. I had a hard time comprehending that if my mom had one, they why did she have the issues she had. "I'm not sure," I said after a while. "Maybe I need to see one."

"Maybe you have."

"Wait a second, what's that word you said before?" I needed to change the subject before I got emotional about my mom.

"What, demons?"

"No, video. What's that?" I asked sarcastically.

"Right? Not in our life." The corners of his eyes narrowed from his grin.

"Do you miss it?"

He gave me the are-you-nuts look. "Every day."

"I can't tell. When I look at you with Raindance"—I softly gestured to the dog— "and I watch you with the other animals, it looks like you like it."

"I love the animals. It doesn't bother me at all to sit with her tonight. I feel useful. So that part you're right about. But animals exist in civilization too."

"Right? Like, this experiment is a little too extreme."

"Totally too extreme."

My gaze fell to Raindance. Her deep breathing was causing her chest to move up and down quickly, but her eyes were completely shut. If I hadn't known she was seriously injured, I'd think she was having the best sleep of her life. I pointed to her and said in a soft voice, "She's sleeping."

His gaze followed my finger, and he too whispered when he said, "Good girl." He stopped rubbing her back, pulled his hand backwards to rest behind him, and turned his face toward me. I see Fulton every day, but he had a new expression on. His lips were in a straight and neutral position, and his chin was slightly angled up. It was as if he'd developed some new maturity. He leaned forward a little more and asked, "What do you miss the most?"

I paused, reflecting on my old life. "Right now, all I can think about is dance. This surgery was such a pain, and I know now I won't be as nimble as I was."

"I thought you had to give it up after you had surgery."

"I'm supposed to, but sometimes when I have feelings of being lost. I don't know what I'm doing out here, but I know if I could just dance, those feelings would go away."

"You'll find something else that does that too. Life's too amazing not to."

A howling echoed in the distance, and it sent a trail of goosebumps to trickle up my spine. "Tell me that was an owl," I whispered as my eyes grew wider, and I checked out the door again.

"That was a really big owl with fangs." He slowly got off the ground and crept over to peer out the door.

"That doesn't help." I giggled nervously as we watched together, but I made sure I was still *behind* him. If some creature was going to come flying in this shed, Fulton would be my shield. He didn't have to know that though.

He dropped a foot to the ground outside and arched his neck to inspect behind the shed. Then he quickly retreated back into the dwelling and said, "You'd better go inside."

I gave him a suspicious look as I was pretty content hiding back here behind him. "You're sacrificing me first, aren't you?"

"You know me too well."

"What about you?"

I didn't even need to ask because as soon as the question was out, his gaze fled right back to the dog. "I'm going to keep Raindance company."

"You're not scared of the fanged owl?"

Putting both hands behind his back, he swept his gaze back outside once more and then cut it back to me. "I can handle it."

I didn't want to leave. I wasn't tired, and even if I was, I wasn't going to sleep. Also, there was something soothing about spending this time with Fulton—just the two of use. Although we saw each other every day, it was rarely like this. Still, the weather was getting worse. Knowing my dad, he'd get up to check the storm and find me out here and suspect the worst. Reluctantly, I unwrapped my blanket from my shoulders and offered it to him. "This will keep you two warm."

"Thanks." A loop-sided smile tugged on the side of his lips, and he took the blanket, being careful to tuck it all around Raindance without waking her. It was pretty surreal to watch Fulton be so kind to Raindance. He had definitely found his element—whatever this is. I turned, taking one step out of the shed, and called back, "See you in the morning."

"Abs," he called after me so softly I barely heard him. I pivoted on one foot, as I was half convinced, I was hearing things.

He stuck his head out the door, and I was able to make out all of his facial features. "I know you don't want to admit it, but I think your parents' experiment is working."

"How so?" My brows furrowed together, as I was unclear what part of this whole experience he was talking about. I'd been through a lot these last months.

"This is changing you." He held a finger up and twirled it around, as to motion to our environment. "And I'm starting to like the new you."

I quickly turned my head away to hide my face. I was so surprised by his sudden compliment that I felt my cheeks grow warm against the chilly air. "Maybe," I mumbled. Then I held up my hand to wave and bee-lined home. I didn't want him to see how big I was grinning.

Chapter Fourteen

"If you would've told me a year ago that I'd be selling home-patched pants to people, I would have said that was gross," I muttered to Fulton. Earlier that morning at the library, I had designed a lilac ballet slipper. I sewed it on the back pocket of a pair of jeans for Lynn's granddaughter while Fulton got his research completed. Now we were on our way to the coffee shop to deliver the pants.

Fulton opened the door to the coffee shop and allowed me to walk in first, not hiding the fact that he was watching me walk. "I'm impressed with how well you're getting around."

"It feels good to be out of bed." I paused as I allowed the scent of roasted vanilla and cinnamon to saturate my senses. Even if I wasn't excited to sew pants, I was looking forward to returning to a coffee shop. It gave me a sense of the modern world I desperately missed.

"I was sort of jealous of you." Fulton trailed behind me as he slowly browsed the rows of home decor items Lynn had set up on shelves. My favorite was the collection of oversized coffee mugs.

There were some in every color, and they had fun coffee puns on them.

"Why would you be jealous of me?" I asked as I leaned around the shelf, trying to see if Lynn was hiding in the backroom.

"Because you didn't have to scoop manure from animal pens and haul it to fertilize the garden."

"They had you on poop patrol all month?" I made a grossed-out face. "I'll never look at garden vegetables the same."

"I agree. That's one of those things you can't unknow. I desperately wish I could go back to not knowing my carrots grow in poop." He made it to the counter and picked up a laminated menu.

As if on cue, Lynn came out of the backroom, wiping her hands on her apron. Seeing us, she smiled. "How are you guys?"

"We're great." I held up the pants to display the patch. "When we spoke on the phone yesterday, you said she was a size eight, so I found these over at that *Fashion for Kids* store downtown. I hope she likes purple."

"Those are awesome. I know she'll love it." She took the pants from me, holding them up to get a better look.

"I hope so." I chewed my lip while she inspected the pants. There wasn't much to the design, so it wasn't hard, but I still felt a little nervous as I waited for her full approval.

The smile lines by Lynn's eyes crinkled when she replied, "They'll make her feel very special."

"If she doesn't like them or if they don't fit, let me know. I know someone who'll take them. I can buy them back from you if need be."

"I'm sure we won't have a problem." She folded them and put them on the back counter, then reached below the counter and retrieved her purse. "What do I owe you?"

I took the store receipt out of my pocket and showed it to her. "The pants were fifteen dollars, and I already had the fabric, so just fifteen."

Lynn dug through her wallet and pulled out a twenty and a ten. "Here's thirty. You should at least double your money in a good business."

"I wasn't doing it as a business. I was waiting for my friend to get done at the library anyway." I motioned to Fulton. "So, I would have been bored if I didn't have this to work on. It was no problem."

She winked at me. "Just say thank you."

"Thank you." I folded the bills in half and tucked them into my pocket.

"Do you need a coffee for the road?" She stood ready to take our order. "Drinks on the house today for you both."

"Now that's an offer I won't refuse," I said as my mouth already watered. "How about a mocha please."

"I'll have coffee with cream and sugar please," Fulton said.

She pointed to the counter stools. "Sit. It'll take just a few moments."

The swivel stool swayed when I climbed onto it, and I steadied myself before I gave Fulton a side-eye. "Are you going to tell me what you learned this morning?"

He plopped down next to me and rubbed his forehead like he was trying to suppress a headache. "Not much of anything," he eventually muttered. "Everything's crazy expensive. I don't know how I'll afford it if I can't stay with a friend."

I rested my chin in my palm, trying to conceal that the thought of him leaving made my heart squeeze tight. Not only was he the only sane person in my life, but he's the only friend I have. Still, I tried to be supportive. "Did you look at jobs?"

"I've applied to several." He emitted an exasperated sigh that was so long, and it fizzled out into a groan. "It's impossible to look normal on a job application when I have no regular method of them contacting me. I can't exactly give them my mom's cell phone number. Plus, entry-level pay in the city barely buys you a drawer to put your socks."

"Have you thought about a different city that's closer to here?" I gestured forward. "I mean, if Brent's moving and your family's here, do you have much to go back to?"

"It's not about going back to my old life. It's more about the way of life in general. I'm not going to live here."

"I feel like that too." I tapped my foot to the beat of the tune playing on the 80s radio station. I may not have been able to dance anymore, but I could still find the beat in a song.

Fulton continued: "I found a couple of people who rent their couches out for like twenty-five dollars a night. I might have to do that for a couple of months until I can find something more permanent. But I will still need money for food and transportation." He sighed heavily and lightly tapped his fingers on the counter as if he was trying to out-do my perfectly on point foot tapping. After a few moments of synchronized tapping, he paused and stared at me until I stopped too. We stared at each other for an awkward moment, and then I laughed because it reminded me of something Becky and I would do. My heart instantly constricted at how much I missed her, so I forced a subject change. "Did you try talking to your parents?"

"They won't help me leave." His lips rolled into a serious expression, and he shook his head vehemently. "This has been their dream forever. They want me to try homeschooling next year, but that's the thing that makes me the maddest. I worked hard at school. I had a four-point-oh, and I deserve to graduate from a real school. I could have been valedictorian this year. They took that from me without thinking twice. They won't help me leave. I get mad just thinking about it because I deserved to graduate with my class."

"I never thought of it like that."

"You never thought about graduating with your class?" He raised a disbelieving eyebrow.

I shook my head. "No. I didn't like school. Honestly, I'm not sure I would've earned a diploma if I had stayed on the path I was going. I spent very little time in school doing actual school. School was more a place for me to show off my latest designer clothes." I pointed to the jeans Lynn had left folded on the back counter. "Which is why this hurts my soul a little to make a craft project out of good fashion."

"If you didn't like school, homeschooling might be a better option for you, but I loathe the idea."

Lynn returned with two to-go cups of coffee and slid them across the counter in front of us. "Here you go."

"Thank you." I took my coffee and pushed the lid down out of habit to make sure it was tight.

Fulton stood up and grabbed his cup. "Thanks, Lynn. And perfect timing because we need to get back on the road." I followed Fulton's lead, but I wasn't ready to go back to the farm. I immediately started counting down the days until I could come back for my checkup. Too many.

Chapter Fifteen

It was exactly two weeks later when I went to see my mom at Evergreen House. My mom cracked her bedroom door slightly ajar and pushed her face into the crack. The hollows of her cheeks caught me off-guard as her dark eyes met mine. She didn't smile. Thankfully, I had come prepared with numb emotions, so it didn't bother me.

"Abs." She opened the door wider and motioned for me to enter.

I took a couple of steps inside, lingering by the door like I was afraid the room was infested with rats. I noticed her room was nicer than the previous ones with modern furniture and carpet, but I wouldn't exactly call it homey. "Happy birthday, Mom." I extended my hand, offering her the bunch of golden wildflowers Millie had helped me pick.

It had been Linda who had discovered the field of newly blossomed flowers in the valley, and she had insisted they would cheer my mom up. I had been careful to cut long stems so they would fit neatly into plastic vase. I thought that was more than what my mom deserved, but Linda, the ever-perfect homemaker, added a personalized touch. Trying to remind my mom of me, she wrapped the jar in glittered fabric tied with an aubergine-colored ribbon around the neck. Linda had meant well, but I knew my mom didn't care about a stupid purple ribbon, *even if it was the perfect shade of aubergine.*

Mom eyed the jar of flowers for a few seconds before accepting them. Just as I had predicted, the look on her face revealed she wasn't impressed. Without giving them a second glance, she set the vase in the center of her coffee table. "They should be nice right there."

"Good. I'm glad they'll work for you," I said, trying to fill the silence. The tension in the room was worse than the most awkward dance partner. I swallowed and pointed to the love seat in her room. "Can we sit?"

"Go ahead." She stood stiffly, as if she was waiting to see if I was actually going to sit.

I plopped down, stretching out both feet. Right before I came here, I had my boots officially taken off, removing all signs of my surgery. Part of me resented that. Now my mom would never see what I went through. The other part of me knew it was better not to care. I wiggled my toes in my flip flops, feeling proud that I could now do that. Then I looked back at her, and I forced myself to sound enthusiastic. "How are you?"

She sat on the couch close enough for me to see her glazed-over eyes. Her body was here, but her mind was off somewhere in heavily medicated land. "I'm great. How are you?"

"Good," I said quietly. I doubted she even heard it. My eyes drifted to her pastel-colored wall décor. I always got a kick out of the decorations in these places because everything was bolted down with silver screws. The maintenance people tried to hide the screws so they would blend in, but if you looked hard enough, you'd see they were there. When I was younger, I made a game of trying to find them all. It was better than having to watch my shell of a mom.

"You're very beautiful today," she said with a plastic smile.

"Thank you." I wanted her words to be sincere, but that's what happened when she was on uppers. It's the only time I ever heard I was beautiful, and she loved me, but she forgot as soon as she came off the medication. "So, what are you up to?"

"I had group this morning. In about an hour they'll serve homemade bread sticks for the residents and guests. Do you want to join me?"

The formality of her tone got to me. I wanted to scream, "I'm your daughter! Will you just for one day treat me like that?" But instead, I said, "That'd be awesome." I had made a commitment to my dad to be there for my mom's birthday. As painful as it was, I forced myself to act engaged for the next two hours.

After my visit, I ambled out to the truck, and I was disappointed to see my dad napping. I tapped on the window. He jerked awake and unlocked the door for me.

"You get a good nap?" I slid inside the truck and closed the door, not hiding the budding annoyance I felt.

"Boy, I was out." His chest moved up as he inhaled a long breath. "How'd it go?"

"Fine," I said tersely. "If you would have come with me, you'd know."

"That's not fair." He gave me his look. "You know her anxiety is worse when more people are in the room. I'll stop in tomorrow, but I wanted your visit to be pleasant since you haven't seen her all summer."

"I know." It was my turn for a deep breath, and I held it for a moment before letting it out. "She was . . . like she usually is when she's in these places. Vacant. We ate breadsticks." I pulled my seatbelt over my lap and clicked it closed.

"That sounds good." He turned the truck on and pulled forward out of his spot.

"It was too awkward to talk so I ate three of them."

He straightened the wheel and then paused to look at me. "Mind if I stop for a coffee before we head back? I need some caffeine."

"That's fine. You can stop at Lynn's place if you want. I wouldn't mind checking to see how her granddaughter liked the pants."

"Sounds like a plan."

Lynn pointed to my bootless feet and squealed, "You're healed!"

I held my hands in the air like I was ready to fly. "I feel like I'm free."

"I bet." She motioned to the counter stools as she moved to position herself behind the counter. "Hop on up."

"Lynn, this is my dad, Cole." I plopped on the same stool I sat on last time and waited for them to exchange pleasantries before I asked, "How did the pants work?"

"She loved them. Now she wants another pair. This time she wants a unicorn. Are you up for another go?"

"Well . . . I don't know." I rested my forearms on the counter and leaned forward. "Maybe one is enough—"

"Sure," my dad interrupted me as he swooped in and took the stool next to me, stealing this conversation right from underneath me by saying, "Abs would love to make another pair."

I glared at him, but he didn't see me, and he kept on blabbering. "Abs can custom make it to just about anything."

"Alisa—that's my granddaughter—was telling me how all the girls on her dance team want a pair too. It would be neat if they all had matching ones. Would that be something you would like to do?" Her inquiring eyes waited for my response.

I felt totally backed into a corner. Before I could reply, my dad told her I would love that. They blabbed for another twenty minutes about me as if I was not standing right there! We ordered coffees to go, and by the time we were back in the truck, I was fuming.

"What a neat lady." Dad steered the truck onto the interstate and whistled a happy tune. My dad never whistles. I gritted my teeth, as I tried to tune it out, but it was no use.

"Why did you do that?" I gripped the door handle to steady myself.

"Do what?" He asked, then right back to whistling.

"Not let me talk."

"I was helping you close the business deal." I held my breath, praying he didn't go back to whistling, and this time he didn't. That's one good thing. I still wasn't happy though.

"I didn't need help," I fumed. "I didn't want to do it. I don't like sewing, and I'm not good at it."

"Now you're being modest. Ever since you were in diapers you've had an eye for fashion. I've worked with enough designers in my life to know when someone has a creative eye."

"I like the design part of it, but I hate sewing. I feel like I have twelve thumbs."

Dad shrugged his broad shoulders. "Well then don't sew it. Just design it."

"You told her I would *make* pants for the whole dance team."

"You're right, I did say that you would make them pants. But I never said you would sew them."

I threw my hands up in the air in frustration. "How am I supposed to make them without sewing them?"

"Think outside the box." He pointed to his forehead. "You can design them and hire someone else to do the sewing. Maybe Linda or Millie—someone who likes to sew."

"Why do you keep ruining my life?" I rubbed my forehead, trying to force this conversation out of my brain.

"I'm trying to help you." His voice leveled up a notch. "I spent my life helping business owners define their businesses, and I know a good opportunity when I see one. There's virtually no startup cost to this, and you could learn business skills and meet people. It doesn't have to be a forever thing, but I think this could be a good hobby for you since you can't dance anymore." *He said it.* The phrase no one had dared to say to me since my first doctor's appointment back in New York. *I can't dance anymore . . .* as in forever. Done.

"Don't worry, Dad." I narrowed my eyes into the tiniest slits. "I'm not going to dance anymore." I desperately wished I had a door to slam, but I settled on staring out the window.

Chapter Sixteen

By the time we got home, I couldn't stand my dad for another second, so I went searching for Fulton. "It's huckleberry season," Fulton explained while he filled up the little red wagon with buckets. "Millie and I are going up the mountain on a hunt. If you want to come, you can."

"Sure, I'd love to come along." Crossing my arms, I stood back and waited for them to get ready.

He frowned at me while he reached behind his head and gave it a nice scratch. "Didn't you just get your walking boots off?"

I looked to the south, studying the path. It didn't look like it was hard. Then I glanced back to my house. It was so small with nowhere to hide. With my dad lurking around, that was the last place I wanted to go. "How far do you plan to go?"

He walked over to the shed and retrieved another bucket that he dropped into the wagon. "Not that far, but I remember how I had to drag you home the last time you came to pick berries."

"Then why did you ask me to come?" I gave him a pointed look, as this conversation was starting to feel almost as annoying as the one I had just completed with my dad.

"I was being polite." An airy chuckle slipped from his lips, pushing them up into a smirk. "I didn't think you'd actually *want* to work, but if you think you can handle it, you're welcome to come. Another person picking berries will make the harvesting go faster."

"I need to get away from my dad for a while," I said softly as I didn't doubt my dad could hear me. "I'll make it work."

He scratched a spot on his arm and looked like he was going to say something in response, but instead he turned toward his house, and yelled, "Millie, let's go."

She appeared at the door of their house, carrying Raindance in both her arms. The dog was obviously too heavy for her to carry, but Raindance didn't seem to mind.

"I don't think so." Fulton pointed to the house. "We can't bring her. She can't even walk well yet. It'll be too much for her."

"She can ride in the wagon." Millie continued to lug the dog forward.

"No, she can't ride in the wagon. The wagon will be full of berries."

"Please!" Millie pleaded. By now, she could barely move forward under the weight of the dog and only slide one toe in front of the other.

"I'm sorry, but I said, 'No.'" Fulton stood still and patiently waited for Millie to accept the bad news.

She reluctantly pivoted and set Raindance on the ground. "Go home, Raindance," Millie sweetly told the dog. "I'll bring you back some huckleberries."

"Thank you." Fulton walked back to the porch, picked up a cooler, made another trip back to the wagon, and set it inside.

Millie saw me standing by the wagon, and her eyes sprang open wider. "Are you coming too?"

"Can I?" I wasn't asking because my mind was made up, but I wanted to see her reaction.

"Sure." Her face brightened up even more. "You can walk with me."

"That's a great idea." I took her hand, and we strolled down the dirt path in front of Fulton, who was left to pull the wagon.

"I think we need to head over west today and go upstream in a zigzag," Fulton called forward. "That way we won't have much of an uphill hike. I saw a couple of different places with huckleberry bushes there. If you start to get tired," he said to me, "we can take a break, but if it gets to be too much, let me know."

"It's gorgeous out," I said, ignoring his caution.

"I bet it feels good. I'd go nuts sitting in the house all day," Fulton said.

"It wasn't too bad. Your mom has been sweet to me. I know more about sewing than I could ever care to know."

"It's not a bad thing to know." He spoke loudly to cover the sound of the wagon rattling in the ruts in the road.

"So, get this . . ." I paused to wait for him to catch up. "Thanks to this little idea you had where you made me seem interested in sewing, my dad now thinks I need to have a sewing business like I'm some grandma."

"Sewing isn't just for grandmas." He held up a point making finger. Once again, he was trying hard to help me, but when it comes to sewing, I wasn't going to be swayed.

"It's not for me."

Fulton slowed as he scanned his gaze left to right to survey the trees, and then he nodded to the left. "Let's sneak through this gap to cross over there. The bushes in the shade tend to yield better." He turned on the path, then something caught his eyes, and he pointed. "Look who's following us."

Before I could turn to look, Millie's eyes popped wider. "Raindance!"

"We'll have to let her catch up now," Fulton moaned. "We don't want her to get lost out here."

Tapping my chin, I thought out loud. "Can't dogs smell their way back?"

"She might be able to, but she'll probably tire out."

Millie scooped the dog up and plopped her into the wagon next to the cooler. I was surprised she found room to lay down. She curled up just as content as can be.

"Why don't we stop over there?" I pointed to some berry bushes I spotted through a clearing. "That way we won't have to drag her further. Fulton let out a sigh, and tossed a look forward, before muttering, "Fine." Then he parked the wagon against a tree, and said, "Millie wanted to have a real picnic, so let's eat first so we can empty out that cooler and have more room for berries."

"My mom and I are going to bake huckleberry pies tomorrow," Millie said as she laid out the contents of the cooler.

"I can't remember the last time I had pie," I said as my brain had a clear image of a nice juicy piece of flaky crust. That sounded so delicious that my mouth watered.

"I was talking to some people in town the other day," Fulton interjected. "Huckleberries are a huge commodity around this part of Montana. My mom wants to try to make a few batches of mini pies to sell. If it does well, she wants to make that one of her businesses." He stretched out on the ground and unwrapped a sandwich.

"What is with everyone and starting all these small businesses?" I griped, remembering my dad's speech that morning. I bit into an apple from the food spread.

"How else do you live off the land if you don't produce something other people want?" Fulton asked.

"It seems like a lot more work than normal jobs, and a lot less money," I said through a mouth filled with apple.

"Maybe, but I think their goal is not about the money anymore. They did that already. They want enjoyment."

I swatted away a fly that had been trying to land on my apple. "Real enjoyable here." Then I pointed to Raindance, who waddled over to rest by Millie's feet. "She loves Millie."

"Yeah, they're best friends. It's funny; she got Sundance the same day, and she hardly looks at her. It's all about Raindance. They go everywhere together."

"I thought dogs were supposed to be *man's* best friend. Shouldn't she be your dog?"

"I'm the one who ran her over, remember?"

"Good point."

"I'm glad they have each other. It'll make it easier for me to leave Millie here."

I knitted my eyebrows together. "I thought you said nothing was working out. Everything was too expensive."

"It is expensive, but I found a solution," he said in a hushed voice so Millie wouldn't hear.

"What's that?" I leaned forward, trying to hear.

"Do you remember that day I was late picking you up from the clinic?"

"Yeah." Instantly my heart picked up a notch as I knew this was about to become a serious conversation.

"I took my GED. I didn't want to tell anyone until I knew how it went, but I got my letter today and I passed. I don't need to go back to high school. I'm going to start community college. I can live in the dorms, plus I'll be eligible for loans. I can work too, since I'll only be taking a few classes."

My mouth felt dry, as that was the last thing I ever expected him to say. Fulton was an excellent student. He loved school. He's the last person I would ever expect to want a GED. I fumbled for words. "How can you take your GED?"

"I started looking into it, and I realized that if I asked my high school to change my status from 'transferred' to 'dropped out,' then I would be eligible to take the GED. I wouldn't need to complete my senior year."

"Why doesn't everyone drop out of school to get their GED if it's that easy?"

"Most people think a high school diploma is a mark of distinction you need for colleges. You are eligible for way more scholarships with it too, and depending on what your goals are, a GED might slow you down. I'm going to spend a year at community college, and I hope to do well enough to then transfer to a state school." He took another bite of his sandwich, and I waited patiently for him to continue. A knot swelled in my throat. I wasn't sure if I was upset at him for finding a way off the farm, or jealous. Whatever it was, I felt ill.

He finally continued, "I turn eighteen at the beginning of the year, so I'll be able to enroll as an adult. Most people aren't adults at the beginning of their senior year of high school."

I pretended to shield my face from the sun, because I didn't want him to see I was getting seriously ill. I had known this was his goal, but I didn't actually think he would achieve it. My stomach tied itself into a giant ball of knots, and somehow, I had broken out into a sweat on my lower back.

This can't be real.

He can't leave me here in Montana all by myself with just Millie and my dad.

My breath went shallow, and I forced an even-toned question, "What are you going to do in college?"

"I want to do something in the science field. I'm hoping once I take a couple courses and talk to my advisor, I can get a clearer picture." He picked up his water bottle. "Another cool thing I learned is that since the last high school I attended was in New York, I'm eligible for in-state tuition. If I would have completed my senior year here, like my parents wanted me to, then I would not have been eligible for that. Once I learned that, I was convinced the best option was to leave now."

"Wow. That's big news. You'll be great at college." I ran a hand though my hair and forced myself to smile even though I felt my stomach slowly sink with each thought Fulton shared with me. It was crazy how he was so open and honest with me too. I'm the only person he trusted to share this with, and I should feel honored, especially after everything we'd been through together, but all I felt was dread.

He can't leave me here.

"I hope so," he chatted away, not picking up on my disappointment. "I know the classes will be tough, but I learned a little about work this summer. I'm also glad we have Raindance because I know Millie will be sad when I leave." Swallowing his last bite of food, he stood up and casually brushed a few crumbs from his shirt before leveling his gaze with mine. "I'm hoping to get enough berries harvested to be able to sell them to pay for my plane ticket."

I let out the quietest breath I could, holding back all my intrusive thoughts telling me that this wasn't fair. "You'd better start picking then."

"I'll help." Millie jumped up and ran to the wagon, grabbed a bucket, and spun on her heel with so much energy, I got a little dizzy. "I'll go down here." She headed into a shaded area behind a row of evergreen trees.

"Stay where we can see you," Fulton stretched his neck out, as his gaze stayed locked on her back.

"Cute!" Millie called back. "You guys, come here, there are baby bears."

My head jolted back. There was no way I actually heard that, but Fulton was already on his feet and bolted toward her, screaming, "Millie, come back!"

I jumped to my feet, slipping in the lose dirt, but I hung back, afraid to see.

It was too late.

Millie had been spotted by Mama bear!

Mama was barreling down directly toward Millie, all while letting out a menacing warning growl. Fulton flicked his gaze back to me for a mere second and pointed down the hill. "Get out of here!" he screamed at me, as he raced to Millie.

I was frozen.

The whole scene played out in slow motion, and it had me in a chokehold. Mama bear leaped down a small cliff and took a giant lunge toward Millie—her claws ready to shred her.

I screamed in horror, throwing my hands forward. "Millie!"

From Millie's side—her forever faithful friend—Raindance, gritted her teeth and sprang forward, hurling herself in front of Millie and latching onto Mama's leg. In a flash, Mama mauled the dog into nothing but fragments. Fulton was next to Millie now, and he threw her behind him with one hand. With the other hand he pulled out his revolver and fired off all the rounds in his gun at the bear, stunning her to stillness. I hadn't even realized I had dropped to the ground, crying hysterically, until Fulton and Millie had circled back around in a hurry to escape.

"Run home!" Fulton screamed as he threw Millie over his shoulder and sprinted. "She's injured, but she's not going to die from her wounds." If there was ever a time to test what my ankles could do, it was now. My legs raced hard, but my mind raced even faster—one swish of a bear paw and Raindance was gone forever. *She had sacrificed herself to save Mill*

Chapter Seventeen

Later that night, I tossed, rolled, fluffed, and huffed through every sleeping position. I was back in my loft bed for the first time in months, and even though my body desperately needed sleep, my mind rejected it. Giving up, I sat up to look out my window. Someone else was losing the sleep battle, and he was pacing back and forth in front of the animal pens.

I wrapped my shoulders in my trusted hug blanket and traipsed to the animal pens. A cloudless sky made the night unusually bright, and I easily found my way and joined Fulton by the fence.

He sullenly looked over at me. "Can't sleep?"

"Nope." I popped the p on the end of the word and shook my head. "Can you?"

"I can't even close my eyes. All I see is that bear thrashing at Millie."

"I'm pretty sure my knees are still shaking even when I lie down."

"I keep playing today over and over in my head." He anxiously ran his hand through the front of his hair. When he was finished, I realized his hair had stayed spiked, like he had been pulling on it—a lot. "I got annoyed with Millie when she wanted to bring Raindance, and then when I said she couldn't come, it's like Raindance knew something was going to happen and came on her own."

"You saved her life, so she gave hers for Millie," I whispered it, because even though it was true, it was still hard to talk about.

His lashes hooded his eyes but hiding his face didn't conceal the how his voice cracked. "It's like I can't shut down my brain. On one hand, I'm mad my parents made us come here and put us in this predicament. I never loathed it like you, but I never wanted to be here. This isn't some wild west show where everyone learns to tame the land. It got real tonight. Millie almost died."

"I know." I swallowed the lump in my throat. I could have never been the one to say those words out loud, and they echoed in the night air.

"So that's one side of my brain." He paused for a moment before continuing. "We can call that the I-want-out-of-here-fast-or-I'm-going-to-lose-my-mind side."

"What's the other part saying?"

He rolled his lips in, shook his head and said, "I can't leave Millie."

"You can't put your goals on hold for her though. She'll be okay. Your parents are here."

"My parents freaked out when they heard about it. And now my mom's forbidding Millie to go back into the woods—ever. I don't even want to go back there. I'd be too terrified."

"See, your parents are smart. They aren't going to let anything happen to Millie. You don't need to worry. Plus, I'm going to be here for a while—unfortunately. So, I'll look after her."

He offered a lopsided grin. "I know you will. You've really become a good friend to both of us."

"I'm trying."

He gestured to his house. "I told them I was leaving."

"What did they say?" I held my voice steady, even though every time he brought up this subject, it tore at my heart a little more. I know it's not personal. If I had a chance to leave, I'd take it, but knowing that, didn't make it easier. I already lost my best friends in New York. I already lost that entire life. He was the one last good thing I was hanging on to, and here he was, slipping away.

"I think they were expecting me to do something," he went on. "My mom was quiet while my dad drilled me about all the details. I knew he would. He was skeptical about my decision to leave high school until I told him my plan was to study pre-veterinary science."

"Wait." I held up my hand to interject. "I didn't know that was your plan."

"It hit me all of a sudden tonight when I was thinking about Raindance and what she did. Then as soon as I thought about it, I knew it was the right path."

"I can see you enjoying working with animals."

"I know, right?" He gestured forward. "It's perfect. Animals are really the only thing that have brought me any happiness this last year."

He didn't intend for his comment to offend me, but it stung. I slid my hand to my chest and held it there. He had been *the one* thing that had made me smile this last year, and I wished he had felt the same way. Swallowing my feelings, I said, "You're going to be a great vet."

"My mom requested I spend my birthday here with the family. She said that if I do that for her, then I had her blessing to follow my path."

"She said that?" I raised an eyebrow in shock.

"I was a little stunned." His lips bent into genuine smile, and it was clear how happy he was to be leaving. Even after losing his dog today, his eyes sparkled back when he spoke about leaving. I wish I could be happy for him.

"It'll be hard to be so far away from my family." He lowered his eyes again and began to trace a line in the dirt with his worn sneakers. "But in a way, seeing what Raindance did for Millie sort of gave me the extra confirmation I needed to know I was on the right path. Now that I have clarity my path involves animal work, I'm excited about it. It completely blows my mind how loyal she was. People aren't like that."

"No, we can be pretty selfish." I watched his perfectly arced line in the dirt get deeper with each pass over it. "You know, I was thinking. Not to change the subject, but what will happen to the baby bears? Will the bears survive if Mama doesn't?"

"I thought about that too. My dad called the park service to report what happened and gave them the information. They're going to check what happened with Mama and see if the cubs need to be moved, or if they'll be able to thrive."

I rocked back on my heel, slowly at first, but when I realized it didn't hurt, I did it a second time. "I guess it's crazy I should be concerned about the cubs . . ."

"It's not crazy. You're changing. I see it every day." After a moment of awkward silence, he wrapped his arm around my shoulders, giving me a friendly squeeze. "I'm proud of you."

I couldn't hold back a smile. *I was changing.* Even if Fulton was the only one who noticed the change, it felt good. "I'm proud of me too," I said. Then we were mostly quiet, but it was a comfortable silence. We stayed like that for a few moments before we parted our ways to try to salvage some sleep before dawn.

Chapter Eighteen

The days quickly ticked away until all that was left keeping Fulton on the farm was a single birthday celebration. Millie energetically tapped on the porch door. "Abs, are you coming to the cookout?"

"Give me one sec. I'm in the bathroom." I applied a layer of my favorite plum-tinted lip gloss, rubbed my lips together, and blotted them with a tissue until it came out the perfect shade. I put the tube into my makeup pouch and placed the bag in the single micro-drawer in the bathroom. I did one last recheck to see how I looked, and then I headed to the kitchen to grab my attempt at a homemade angel food cake. Since I wasn't much of a baker, I was proud of it, even if it did come out a tiny bit lopsided. "Can you grab this cake from me?" I asked Millie. "I'll bring the fruit topping."

"Sure." She entered the house and willingly freed my hands. "I like your hair down like that."

"Thanks. I usually like it out of my face, but I thought I'd try something different tonight since it's a party."

Her eyebrows lifted. "Aren't you excited?"

"I am." With forced enthusiasm in my voice, I balanced the fruit bowl and shut the fridge. Then I opened the door for her and followed her outside.

"There she is." Eddie pointed to me. "We're starving."

"You didn't have to wait for me." I set my bowl down on the long table that had been set up outside and plopped down on a lawn chair. "It looks like we're still missing the birthday boy."

"He was here, but he got tired of waiting for you girls, so he went to take a nap," Eddie replied.

"What?" I knitted my eyebrows together and cut my gaze back to his house.

"Kidding." Eddie grinned, showing off his trilogy of silver crowns on the bottom row of his mouth. "He went to get more plates."

Linda looked up at me from where she was slicing a smoked brisket. "Don't mind him. He is just hungry."

"I am hungry," Eddie defended. "We worked hard all summer, so we deserve a day off to feast."

"I never said you didn't." Linda placed the tray of brisket in the center of the table. "I think we're ready to eat. The brisket came out with just the right level of moisture. Not too dry." She sat down next to Eddie.

"There he is." Eddie pointed toward Fulton, who was carrying a stack of plates with silverware stacked on top. "I knew you took a nap."

"No nap. I couldn't find any forks, so I had to wash some." He set the plates in the only empty corner of the table. "Nice that I have to do dishes on my birthday."

"You're eighteen," Eddie said. "You get to do everything for yourself now."

"Oh no," Linda interrupted. "Even though you're an adult, I'm happy to help you."

Eddie pointed at Fulton with his fork. "Sit down already so we can eat."

"You're like a vulture." Fulton squeezed in the last chair to fit at the table. "I'm here. Eat."

"First, before we do"—Linda held up her glass— "I want to make a toast."

"Are you kidding me?" Eddie complained with a smile. "Actual vultures are going to smell my brisket and get it before I do."

"Stop it, now." Linda playfully elbowed Eddie before raising her glass again. Her eyes focused on Fulton. "I want to tell you that I'm proud of you. This day came way too soon. It's been an absolute joy to see you grow into the man you are. I love you. I wish you all the best as you move to college tomorrow."

"Aw, thanks, Mom." Fulton picked up his glass and held it up.

"And happy birthday," she added. She pushed her glass forward, clinking it with Fulton's. "Cheers."

We all clinked glasses and repeated, "Happy birthday." A knot swelled in my throat, as nothing about wishing Fulton off to college felt good, but I wasn't going to ruin his special day. If anyone deserved to go to college, it was him. Even if it meant, he was leaving me behind.

"Can we eat now?" Eddie aimed his fork at the brisket, getting ready to stab at a piece of meat.

"Yes." Linda did one final toss of the vegetable salad and passed it to Fulton.

My dad passed a basket of cornbread muffins around the table and said, "I made a bean bag toss game for when we're done eating—if anyone wants to step up to the challenge, that is."

Fulton helped himself to salad and then passed it to my dad. "You mean cornhole? I'll play. I'm awesome at cornhole."

"I should warn you that bean bag toss is my game," my dad said.

"I'm not scared," Fulton said, and then left out a chuckle.

"That's your first mistake."

Eddie snickered. "I can take you both down. I've never lost a bean bag toss match."

"Have you even played bean bags?" Linda asked Eddie while she eyed the mountain of brisket he had heaped onto his plate.

"You're going to find out here shortly that bean bags are my superpower."

"I'm shaking," my dad teased. He shifted his gaze to me. "You're quiet. Everything okay?"

No, I'm not okay.

A year ago, you could have never convinced me I'd be sad about saying goodbye to Fulton Rogers, but inside my chest, my heart was pounding so hard, I feared if I didn't get relief soon, my heart would crack. It took all my strength to fake a smile. "Just tired from baking all day."

"Well, we are glad you did." Linda smiled reassuringly at me. "I think your cake looks beautiful."

"Thanks." I hardly managed to look at her, but instead lowered my gaze, and picked at my corn muffin.

Millie knelt on her chair, reaching her arm over to the side. "I'm ready to try a piece of cake."

My stomach squeezed tight, at the thought of already moving onto the cake. Once we eat my cake, the night is over. *It's goodbye.* My chin quivered, but I couldn't sit here and be exposed. Desperate to step away from the table, I stood and said, "I'll get some bowls."

Linda put her hand on mine, before I was able to slip away from the table. "Don't worry about it. I got it taken care of. You just eat. I'll dish it up." She stood up, still holding her hand on mine like she was trying to hold me down. I let my body sink back down into my chair, which must have satisfied her, because she released my hand and asked, "Anybody else ready for cake?"

"I'll take some." My dad held his fork up like he was voting.

"I'm ready for my presents." Fulton sat back in his chair, eyeing the cards in front of him.

"We're doing this backwards, aren't we?" Linda handed Millie her bowl. "We're supposed to sing, do presents, and then cut the cake, right?"

"No singing," Fulton said. "Let's skip to the cake and presents."

Linda handed Fulton a bowl of cake, and with her other hand she slipped him an envelope. "Happy birthday."

He took the envelope and ripped it open. I could see a stack of hundred-dollar bills pressed inside the card. He read it quietly then folded it back up. "Thank you, guys. This means a lot to me. I'll need it when I get to New York."

"We figured you would want money," Eddie said.

"It's perfect," Fulton said. "That'll definitely help me out until I get a job."

"Since you're officially a college boy tomorrow," Linda said, "I don't see why you can't have access to your college fund. Your dad and I talked, and we're going to take care of this year's tuition and boarding for you."

Fulton's eyes widened. "Really? That's awesome. Thank you."

"We want you to have time to study and do well. We hope this helps you have more time to balance everything."

Fulton leaned over and hugged his mom. "Thanks. It means a lot to me that I have your support."

"We're proud of you. And we want you to come back to see us occasionally too."

"I'll definitely come visit." Fulton stuffed the card back in the envelope and tucked it under his bowl so it wouldn't blow away.

Millie pushed a tiny red box toward him. "Open mine."

Fulton lifted the lid and removed the tissue paper. Then he dug inside to finally discover a braided string.

"It's a friendship bracelet I braided from embroidery thread," Millie said.

"You did a nice job. Thank you." Fulton rolled it between his fingers, looking at the blue and red threads twisted together.

"That way you can't forget about me," Millie said.

"I'd never forget about you." He wrapped it around his wrist, pinching it closed. "Can you help me tie it?" He held his arm in front of her.

Millie tied it in a double knot, and when she was finished, she was beaming. "I think I'm going to be a designer like Abs."

"First of all, I'm not a designer. So, jot that down," I joked.

My dad grinned at me then reached his hand in the opposite direction to give Fulton a card. "This is from Abs and me."

Fulton eagerly opened it to find more money. "Thanks, you guys. I appreciate it."

"You're welcome," my dad said.

"If my dad allows me to, I'll come visit you." I snuck a sideways glance at my dad.

"Sure, you would," my dad said without missing a beat. "You'd go in his suitcase tomorrow if I didn't check it." My dad wrapped his arm around my shoulder. "Remind me to check your suitcase," he said to Fulton.

"I'd even have room in my suitcase since I gave away all my possessions last year," Fulton said with a smile.

"I can't wait any longer." Eddie stood up. "I ate so much brisket that my superpowers are busting out of me." He flexed his chest forward, posing like Superman. "Who wants to team up with a bean bag champion?"

"Let's do this." Fulton set his card down and stood up. "Alright, everyone. Off your butts. It's game time."

Chapter Nineteen

Later that same night, Linda gathered the last of the party debris. "I'd better get all this garbage put away before the bugs come out. Millie, can you take that wash bucket into the house?" She pointed to the overflowing bin of dishes.

Millie yawned and obliged. "I'm ready for bed." She followed her mom inside the house. My dad had disappeared over an hour ago when his full stomach started calling him to a nap. Eddie stood and folded the chair he had been sitting on. "You want to help me load these chairs back into the shed?" he asked Fulton.

Everyone had a chore to busy themselves with but me. I wasn't ready to go inside my house yet. The night had evened out to the perfect summer temperature, and although I would never admit it to a single living soul, the early autumn view of the mountains was captivating.

I made my way to stand under my mom's pergola. She had seen a picture of one just like it in an architecture magazine, and my dad had insisted on building it for her the first week we were here. He wanted her to have someplace beautiful just for her. She had talked about how she wanted to plant grape vines at the bottom so they would wrap the wood beams in a coat of colors. No one told her it would take a minimum of three years for the grapes to get established in this northern state. Thus, the beams were still naked, echoing my mom's absence.

I'm not sure why I missed her; maybe I didn't really ever miss her, but I missed the idea of her, of what our relationship could have been if things had been different. The sun had started to set behind our mountain, painting other-worldly hues of violet, rose, and gold waves across the sky. I savored every moment until the last glows dissipated like dying embers.

"Good, I was hoping you hadn't gone inside yet."

I turned to see Fulton jogging toward me. As much as I knew this was going to be the last chance we had to talk to each other, I pinched my lips together, already regretting it.

Sure, I was happy that he was happy but that's where my happiness stopped. Inside I was dying. I turned away from him, staring out into the sky, "It was a beautiful night."

Fulton scanned the mountain skyline with so much ease, I could tell he no longer resented being here. I guess that's what happened when you have your plane ticket out of here already in your pocket. "As much as I am excited to get back to the city, I will miss this view. It's an unexpected beauty."

I felt the familiar sting of a mosquito and slapped my arm, defeating it. "I could do without the bugs." I brushed the bug glue from my arm.

"It's going to rain later tonight, so I'm sure they're going to start to come out thick."

"I suppose." I sighed and slid a foot back toward my house. "I was just thinking I'd better get inside and check on my dad."

"He'll be fine." Fulton waved my concern away with one hand, flashing something he was holding. "Nothing a little sleep won't cure."

"What do you have?" I pointed to his hand.

"It's something I wrote that I wanted to share with you." He held it out, and slowly unfolded it. "When I decided to go to vet school, I started looking at the entrance requirements, and it's going to be pretty competitive."

"I bet." Just then the wind picked up, whipping my hair in front of my eyes so I couldn't see. It was like the wind mimicked the emotional turbulence I was about to experience. I swept my hair to the side to keep it out of my face. "But it'll be worth it because it'll be a great job for you. Who doesn't love a vet?"

"I hope it works out," Fulton said. "Anyway, I noticed all the applications require an essay or two. Most of the topics are about why you want to be a vet or what makes you a good fit for the program. I started working on it a little this week to see what I could come up with."

"You're such an overachiever." I grinned teasingly at him.

"Not really an overachiever. More of an over-stresser."

"You don't need to stress out."

"I'm trying not to. But anyway, at first, I was going to write about my entire experience of moving here and what I learned from working with the farm animals. Then I decided to narrow the essay's thesis to be on what I learned from Raindance." His eyes were wide with vulnerability when he handed me the letter. "I thought you'd want to read it."

I grabbed it and was immediately drawn to the title: *Wisdom I Learned from Raindance*. I smiled. "Is this the whole essay?"

"No, I wrote out the whole incident of how I ran her over, how I, a stranger to her, got to be the one to comfort her when she was at the vet, and how she died. This is part of the end."

"I didn't know you're a writer." I skimmed the contents of the page.

"I'm not, but ever since the accident, I can't sleep at night, and there isn't much you can do in a tiny home that won't wake people up." He pointed to the sheet. "Read it."

I started to read and came across a list:

1. Never be afraid to help a friend. You'll always get more than you give.

2. Be fearless—better to die a hero than to live to old age as a coward.

3. Sometimes God gives you a gift, but in order to get your attention he needs to disguise it as an accident.

4. Believe in angels.

I let my index finger linger over the last one. Those were the words I had thought a hundred times. "She was our angel, or at least a little angel's helper." I looked back at him.

"Doesn't it explain why she was in our life for such a short time? Plus, she took to Millie so quickly like she knew she had a job to do. I can't stop thinking about how I wasn't going to let her come with us."

"Don't even think about that. It was meant to be." I folded the sheet back up and offered it back to him. "Thanks for letting me read that."

"You keep it. I mean, if you want it."

"I do." I refolded it and tucked it into my back pocket. It would be a nice reminder of Raindance.

"It's weird. You've been in my life for as long as I can remember, but it's been the last few months that I've finally gotten to know you," Fulton said as he took a small step forward.

"Unwillingly at first." I did my best to smile sweetly even though every ounce of it felt fake. I was sad. Really sad. And jealous.

"I'm glad. I mean, I'm not glad we had to be dragged all the way out here, but I think that's one of the few bonuses I've found to this whole experience. I got to know the real you."

"I would be lying if I said I wasn't super jealous you're leaving."

"Well, after eighteen years, we finally formed a truce. Isn't that funny?"

"I guess it's better than parting as enemies, but I'm happy for you. Good luck." I leaned in and gave him a fast, friendly hug. When he pulled away, I said, "I'd tell you to email or call, but you know I can't do those fancy things."

He chuckled. "It's going be weird to have freedom like that again." His grin fell when he saw my lips didn't even waver towards a tiny smile. "What's wrong?"

I lowered my eyes. "I keep thinking that it stinks you're leaving. I'm going to miss you."

"Don't be sad."

"I'm happy for you." I forced another smile, but it must have looked pretty cheesy and unbelievable because it only made him crack a bigger smile.

"Don't worry." He reached out, touching my forearm, causing me to turn toward him, which was something I'd been avoiding doing. I didn't want to have to look directly at him. Just as I pictured, there was so much excitement swirling around in his eyes. It was clearly one of the happiest days of his life. "Your turn to leave will come soon," he added.

"It can't come fast enough. Living here is terrible when we were stuck here together, but now that I see you get out, it just makes me feel more stuck. I want to leave too."

"It can feel like an austerity." He lowered his eyes for a moment before reaching his hand out. "Come on. Dance with me."

Wrinkling my nose, I cut an angled glance back at him as this was a crazy request. "Why?"

"You told me you dance to move through the bad stuff," he said.

"Yeah, bad stuff, but this is beyond bad."

"Come on, don't be scared of my clown feet. One dance. All my life I've watched from the shadows while you danced, but I've never got to dance with you."

I was at a loss for words, so I reluctantly took his hand and stepped forward. I kept my face tucked close to his chest because I didn't want to look at him. I bit my lip, trying to avoid the tenderness of the moment, and I let my eyes close. I instinctively felt the gentle nudges from Fulton, and I moved to align my feet with his. I danced, and I prayed that it would be a good enough diversion to get me through this goodbye.

Maybe it was the movement, or the moment, but I was vastly aware that this was the first dance I'd even attempted since my surgery. It wasn't classical ballet, and my former dance-snob self would have struggled to even call it a dance, but together we wove a sort of amorphous thing—a thing that became a moment, and a moment that couldn't help but bring back other moments. All of my big dance moments came flooding back: the first time I stepped up to a barre, discovering I was a twirler, all the years of hard work. Everything funneled through my head, creating a patchwork of dance memories. My body flowed, and so did my memories. And then, as my memories slowed and came to a stop, so did my feet. I opened my eyes to find Fulton staring at me with a look of concern.

He raised an eyebrow. "Did you hear me?"

"Um, no, what? Sorry. Did you say something?" His soft laughter was layered in disbelief, and he shook his head. "No, it's fine. I could tell something was going on in your head." Then he looked at me with one of the most serious looks I had ever seen on his face. I bit down even harder on my lip, thinking the moment was about to turn awkward, but it didn't. It got softer. Then he said, "You're going to be fine here in your exile, and I'll be back to see you at Christmas."

"That's forever."

"I know it feels like that, but it will go fast." He briefly glanced at the fading sun. "I'd better go in. I want to say goodbye to Millie tonight, and it looked like she was ready for bed when I came out here."

"You better get in there then."

He held up his hand in a wave. I copied his wave and watched him walk away. Right before he went into the house, he turned and said, "Keep dancing." I held up my hand again and I was fully ready to wait as he disappeared inside for good, but my feet shuffled forward, not stopping until I had closed to gap between us.

"What?" He raised a brow, forming a puzzled expression. I didn't have any words to give him. Instead, I rose to the tips of my toes, tilted my chin up, and pressed a chaste kiss to his lips. As soon as our lips met, my heart slammed against my ribcage, and Fulton stood frozen, doing nothing to kiss me back.

With instant regret, I dropped to my flat feet again. My cheeks flamed warm, and I just couldn't look at him as I spun on my heel and headed back to my house. "Abs," Fulton's low voice called after me, I blocked it out as I entered my house and slammed the door behind me. *I couldn't believe I did that.* I ran my hand through my hair drawing in a deep breath, trying to forget about the last minute, but something had changed. Something was happening to my heart. It was twisting inside me, acting like I was about to have some sort of health emergency. I flattened my palm against my chest and felt my heart pounding fiercely. This was a new sensation that hadn't been there before—*a pull*.

Chapter Twenty

The next morning met me like fog during a beach vacation. I was disoriented in my thoughts, clumsy in my actions, but I was clear on one thing: Fulton was gone.

I brushed my hair back into a ponytail, but I got annoyed when I couldn't get the bumps to smooth out. "Dad!" I called from the bathroom.

"What?" He was sitting on the couch, leisurely sipping his morning blend of coffee.

"Are you going to town today?"

"Yep, going to pick up Kanoo."

I tilted my ear toward the door, straining to hear better. "You're getting a canoe?"

"No, I'm going to go pick her up."

I dropped my hairbrush, wove my way through the kitchen, which was now expertly boobie-trapped with boxes of canned preserves we had prepared for winter, and stood in front of him. "What about a canoe?"

"I'm going to get her.""Who is she?"

"It's my new Jersey cow. Her name is Willameena Kanoo."

"You're getting a cow?"

He flashed an exhausted expression. "I'm so sick of goat milk, goat yogurt, goat cheese, and goat cream. If I have another goat concoction, I think I'll vomit." He said the word vomit forcefully like he was warning me to step back.

"Well, at least we finally agree on something about this place."

"Yep, I thought it might grow on me, but I can't do it anymore. Fulton did a lot of research on Jersey cows. They have a special kind of milk called A2 milk. It's supposed to be the best for human consumption. He found Kanoo for sale, and as soon as he told me about her, I knew I was officially done with the goat milk—forever. The owner's going to meet me in town today. You want to ride with?"

"Can I? I want to get a haircut." I paused when he didn't immediately approve my request. "Or is that too modern for us mountain people?"

He looked at me with a humored look. "No, you can get a haircut. I was thinking how nice it might be to get one too."

"That's two things we agree about." I paused and gave him a look of warning. "Should I press my luck for a third and ask for internet service?"

He stood up and reached behind the sofa, retrieving something. "Well, you don't have to press your luck. I was going to wait to tell you about this until next week, but I might as well let you know about it now." He handed me a flat box.

I suspiciously flipped the lid opened to find a new laptop. "Are you kidding, Dad!"

He held up his hand. "Just wait. Don't get too excited. You need it to do your schoolwork on."

"Does it work?"

"Yes, it works. The more I looked into your home-study school, the more I realized it was going to be a huge pain to not have your own laptop. Your assignments need to be uploaded, and you are required to participate in online discussions. So, this is a gift, but it comes with boundaries. It's only for school."

I took it out of the box and held it on my lap. It was beautiful. So sleek and smooth. Like a child with a stuffed bear, I hugged it. "I love it. Thank you, Dad."

"You're welcome. Now put it back in the box. I'll get you the login information for school later, and we'll get your account set up."

I was ahead of him already. I eagerly packed it up and placed it safely on the bookshelf. Then I obediently went to the door and slipped on my shoes. "Meet you in the truck," I called as I ran outside.

My dad always kept his keys tucked inside the sun visor flap on the driver's side. I inserted them and cranked the ignition so I could listen to the radio while I waited for him. I was bobbing my head to some 80's station when he slid in next to me. "So, we're meeting this farmer at noon. That'll give us more than a couple hours for haircuts. I think there's a walk-in place right downtown, so it should be easy." He shifted the truck into drive and carefully maneuvered around the growing web of animal pens in the yard.

After driving in silence for a few moments, he stole a sideways glance at me. "You look like you're in a good mood."

"Best day ever."

"What would you think about stopping in to see your mom first? It won't take long. I need to check on her since I haven't yet this week."

"I guess if I have to," I moaned, my mood instantly plummeting. I dropped my eyes to the hem on the bottom of my shirt. The thread had started to unravel, and since Linda had trained me so well, I instinctively stuck my finger in a hole by the seam to examine how I could fix it.

The wheels crackled on the gravel when my dad turned onto the road. "Do you need some money for new clothes?"

Shocked at the gesture, I looked up. He pointed to my shirt hole.

"I'm not going to say no."

"We can probably make a stop for that before we head home."

"You're starting to scare me." I narrowed my eyes to study his side profile because nothing about this day was making sense. "You are too agreeable to all the things I'm not supposed to be having."

"It was sort of a cleanse for the summer to get rid of everything. But now that we've done without for a while, I don't see the harm in adding some things back in with moderation."

"I'm stunned." My jaw fell open.

"It was more your mom's deal that we go to this level of extreme, but it looks like she's not coming home for a while, so what she doesn't know can't really hurt her, right?"

"That seems dishonest."

"I don't think it is. We could tell her about it. Although, I don't think she's in the right frame of mind to care about that stuff now." He completed the final turn onto the highway and accelerated. "Anyway, what's going on with your jeans thing?"

"It's not a jeans thing."

"I think it could easily be." He spoke louder, competing with the road noise.

"I don't really want it to be a thing."

"You don't like money?"

"I do, but you won't let me spend it on anything I want to buy, so what's the point?"

"Because you're going to be seventeen here shortly. Most kids your age have a job. This could be a nice little side business for you."

"Patching people's jeans?" I flashed him my grossed-out face.

"No, designing patched jeans. It's a whole different market."

"I don't see how that has a market."

"Everything has a market; you just have to know how to reach it. That's my job. I'd help you there."

"So, what's my market? People who want to upcycle their used jeans?"

"If I were you, I'd start a new line of your own."

I gave my dad a warning look as there was a niggling in the back of my head saying this might have already gotten way out of hand. "Did you talk to Lynn about this already?"

"I might have stopped in to have coffee when I was in town."

"Why would you even bring this up?" I turned sideways to get a good look at him. I had to see his face to see if he was serious or not. His jaw was closed, but all the lines on his face were relaxed.

He was enjoying this!

"I think this could be a neat thing for you. Winter's long. You need something to do. Plus, you're good at it. You have an eye for color, and you're good at visualizing the results."

I held my hands to the sides of my face and made a noise like I was about to rip out my hair. "I don't think you listen when I talk. I have said it so many times! I don't like to sew."

He held his hand up like he was trying to push my attitude down. "I heard you." He spoke softer. "I wouldn't take that approach. I'd look into wholesale and order new jeans direct from the warehouse. You would be able to be a part of the design process, and then we could start small with some samples at Lynn's store to see what the kids like."

"I don't know how to do any of that," I said quietly, slowly realizing my dad had been doing research that I hadn't been aware of. Part of me felt betrayed. The other part was intrigued.

"I do. I've worked with hundreds of designers." My dad took the exit off the highway onto main street, heading toward Evergreen House, and picked up where he left off, "I've helped build many brands, and they are all the brands you willingly spend hundreds of dollars on. And guess what? Those designers aren't any more talented than you are."

"I do love to shop," I confirmed with a blank expression, trying to avoid accidentally letting my dad think that I thought he had a good idea.

"This is a way to make a passion your job. It's easy to start a business when you're young because you have no one else to depend on you for money. You should think about it. You might need a distraction *now*."

I furrowed my eyebrows. "What do you mean now?"

He sighed. "I mean that you're going to be bored now that summer's over. Your school won't take long. You've always had dance classes to fill your time, but you can't do that anymore. You know, your mom's not home, and now Fulton's gone . . ." His voice trailed off like he knew he had said too much.

It should've bothered me that he reminded me I couldn't dance and my mom was sick. I was able to brush those away easily. The thing that burned the most was that he reminded me Fulton was gone, like somehow, I'd managed to forget, which I clearly hadn't. It just cut deeper when he mentioned it again. I swallowed, forcing my emotions down and turned to stare out the window.

My dad pulled into the shaded parking lot of Evergreen House. We walked together in silence through the front door. Standing by the nurses' station was a nurse who smiled when she recognized my dad. "Good morning, Cole. How are you today?"

"It's a good day. Can't complain. Is Claire available?"

"I'm still waiting for her to get up. I haven't been able to stop in with meds yet." She looked at her watch. "You know, it's after nine. I should check on her and make sure she's feeling well. I'll walk you back." She waved for us to follow her down the carpeted corridor.

"Do you want me to go in or wait in the hall?" I whispered to my dad as we walked.

"Let's see how's she doing. I'll go in first. If she's in a good mood, I'll wave at you."

The nurse stopped at my mom's room, tapping lightly on the door. When no one answered, she opened it slightly and peeked her head in. Then she turned back to us and whispered, "She's still in bed." She slowly pushed the door open wider and signaled for us to wait by the door. She approached my mom from the foot of the bed and lightly touched her feet, still covered with a blanket. A funny look came over her face, and she quickly reached for the top of the blanket and folded it back, revealing it had been stuffed with pillows. My mom wasn't there. A look of alarm flashed across her face as she pulled the blanket all the way off.

I looked at my dad blankly and said, "She ran away again."

Chapter Twenty-One

I peered through the passenger window of the truck, straining my eyes for clues. "Look for water."

"You thirsty?" Dad asked while his eyes stayed glued to the streets.

"Not that kind of water. Like, environmental water. Whenever she runs away, she's found near water. Remember that time she escaped Bellevue? We found her down by the docks."

"Now that you mention it, I remember another time when she was found near the pond in Central Park."

"Told you."

"What made you think of that?"

"I just noticed a pattern, so I thought I'd mention it. Remember the time she was on the Brooklyn Bridge?"

"I never realized there was a pattern. I wonder why?"

"Cause she's crazy. She doesn't need a why."

My dad turned the truck to head down a back street. Slowing down, he turned me, and said, "I wish you wouldn't say those things about her."

"That she's crazy?" One of my brows quirked higher than the other as I saw nothing wrong with it. "It's true."

"There's a nicer way to talk about it. Did you want to be called crippled when you were walking around with both feet in casts?"

"My surgery was a completely different deal. That was over and done in a matter of months. Mom's been crazy my whole life."

"She's not crazy."

"What do you call her?"

"The doctor said she was having a bout of depression."

"This week," I snap back. "It's like a different diagnosis each day of the week. The Monday doctor says she has borderline personality disorder, the Tuesday doctor says she's a giant skitzo, then Wednesday's doctor comes around and says she's full of baloney and faking it, but by Thursday it'll be PTSD—"

"That's enough!" My dad slammed his fist onto the steering wheel. "I know this is hard on you." He yanked at the steering wheel, swerved the truck to the side, and slammed on the brakes, stopping the truck at the end of the street. He killed the engine with an exaggerated motion showing his frustration. "Look, this isn't easy for anyone. But she's your mother, and you making fun of her illness and the struggles she has gone through to get a diagnosis doesn't help any of it. She needs help."

I pushed my face into my hands, trying to release the pressure in my brain. After a moment, I came up for air. "But all we've ever done is try to help her! How many times has she been in therapy or at some clinic or some home, or hospital, or even this move? It's never-ending. When's it going to work?"

Dad inhaled deeply, taking a few measured breaths, then calmly said, "You know, I haven't done this farming thing long, but there's an expression that rings true for this that I'm sure you've heard of: 'You can bring a horse to water, but you can't make it drink.' We've been bringing her to get help, but we can't make her receive it. She has to do that."

I chewed my thumbnail quietly while I digested my dad's analogy. "Has she ever been normal?"

"It's hard to say. I didn't know her very long before we got married. Then we got pregnant right away. I noticed things were a little off then, but I thought it was pregnancy hormones. Then you came along, and the doctors said it was post-partum. I guess, now that I look back, she's always had a cycle."

"So, she's always been like this?"

"I'd say so."

"So, there's a good chance she'll always be?"

My dad slowly nodded his head.

"Then if all we're doing is leading her to useless water she'll never drink, when do we get to start living our lives the way we want instead of wasting all this effort?"

"We can't give up on her. That's not what family does."

"We don't have to give up. But we don't have to be so drastic if we know she won't get any better. She wasn't any better or worse in New York. This move didn't help. It made things worse. So why can't we move back? Then she can see the doctors who already know her."

"I don't have answers. Maybe we will at some point. I can't defend this move anymore, at least not right now." He laid his head back on the headrest and closed his eyes. I watched the crow's feet by his eyes deepen as he closed his eyelids. For the first time ever, I felt sorry for my dad.

It was like I had a bird's eye view of what my life had been and how my dad had tried desperately to be the glue that kept my mom from cracking wide open. He didn't know how to raise a daughter. He'd failed miserably all the time, yet he was the one who was here now. I don't even know if he wanted to be here. This move had been my mom's deal. Now that I thought about it, I had no idea what my dad even wanted out of this life. He never said. Or maybe he had said but I never cared. I felt an unusual stinging in my heart that I hadn't felt for my dad before. It was unpleasant but not painful. It made me want to care what he wanted.

After searching fruitlessly for hours, he dropped me off back home sometime after dark. As far as I knew he wasn't going to come home until he found her. I, on the other hand, was numb to her. At least that's what I told myself.

The next day, I awoke and found that my dad still hadn't come home, but it didn't make me sad. I wandered outside and found Millie brushing Sundance's tail. She had already tied a rainbow-colored ribbon on the top of it, and from the look of the pile of bows by her feet, she had big plans for the rest of the makeover.

I approached them. "She's sure tame."

"Fulton said it was because she was too old to care, but I think she likes me." Millie carefully pulled the brush all the way through to the end of Sundance's tail, getting every strand. As soon as the brush was out, Sundance would sweep her tail away in the opposite direction, messing up her perfect tail. Millie giggled. "She likes to play too."

I held my hand palm up for Sundance to smell. She lightly brushed her nose over it. Once she got used to me, I lifted my hand to pet the top of her head. "Pretty girl."

"You want to brush her?" Millie held the brush out.

I took it and very gently eased it through her mane. "That's a sweet girl," I said. She swept her tail again, messing up my grooming. "I can see why Fulton likes the animals. It's pretty cool when you can see they trust you."

"She likes you," Millie said. "You have a new friend."

"Good," I said sort of down-heartily. "I could use one."

"What's wrong?" I could feel her eyes graze over my face.

"I feel sad. Sort of empty." I wasn't sure why I was telling Millie this. Maybe it was so built up inside me that I couldn't hold it in anymore. As always, and perfectly on cue, sweet Millie wrapped her arms around my waist to hug me.

"It's okay. You're doing okay."

"Am I?" I sniffed.

"I think so."

I felt slightly better when she said that, but I was also amused that an eight-year-old girl could give me advice to make me feel better.

"We can share her." Millie nodded toward her pony. "She always cheers me up. You're welcome to sit with her whenever you want."

I wished a pony could make everything better. "Thank you," I said. "You're a sweetheart."

The sound of tires rolling over gravel broke the air. I looked up to see my dad's truck pulling into the yard, and the passenger seat was occupied. My mom was in the truck.

Millie pointed when she saw the same thing I did. "Look, Claire's home."

I froze. "This can't be good."

"She must be better."

"Go in the house." I stepped in front of her as if I was trying to shield her from an attacker.

"But—"

"Please, honey. I'll come get you later and we can hang out. My mom might not be ready to see you yet." The smile she had been wearing slowly trickled away until it was gone. She turned on her heel and trudged to the house, leaving me standing with Sundance.

I watched the pickup roll to a stop. My dad hopped out of the vehicle and hurried to meet my mom on the passenger side. As she got out, my mom turned her head and saw me. I held y breath, waiting. Then I saw her fuzzy unibrow. She was in her mood—the one her personality disorder therapist called splitting.

"Come on, Claire." My dad held out his hand, trying to grab hers, but she shook it off. "Let's go in the house, hon." He reached behind her waist, trying to guide her forward.

She pushed his hand down, focusing her attention on me, and called, "Aubergine."

My dad gave me one of those looks like he was trying to avoid looking at a car accident. He again tried to wrap an arm around my mom's waist to divert her into the house, but she walked out of it.

"Aubergine." As she got closer, I could see her eyes were glazed over, but not how they got from medication. This was how they looked when she was in her alternate reality. I waited for her to tell me all the reasons why I made her life suck today.

"Hi, Mom," I squeaked out, stiff shouldered like I was afraid to take up space.

"What are you up to?" she asked accusingly.

I shot a look over to my dad, who promptly placed a hand on her shoulder, redirecting her. "Let's go in the house. It's getting late."

She planted her feet on the ground. "I want to know."

"She's not up to anything," my dad said.

This was the phase she went into when everything was *my fault*. Her therapist said I had become her trigger person. I backed away, looking to my dad for help. I didn't feel sorry for him anymore. This had to be one of the most irresponsible things he'd ever done. I leveled my gaze with him, demanding answers, "Why'd you bring her home?"

His gaze bounced from me, to mom, and then back to me. With a defeated voice, he said, "I didn't know what else to do."

"You know how she is when she gets in this mood." I gestured forward, not caring that she can hear me talk about her. She more than likely won't remember any of this anyway. "She's not going to let up on me."

"She's sick." Dad's stern reply only infuriated me more because he was clearly not seeing how this isn't going to work for either of us. Mom needed care, and she was not getting that here, and while she's here, she's going to make my life miserable.

"You're choosing her." I narrowed my eyes, wishing just one time he would think about how this was for me. "There's nowhere for me to hide. Unless you want me to sleep in the truck . . ." When he didn't say anything, I got yelled, "You brought her here. You can figure this out!"

My dad wrapped both arms around her waist tightly and started to tug her away from me. "She's not ready to go back to Evergreen yet," he called back. "I need some time to figure something else out."

"And in the meantime, your daughter gets to do what?" I threw my hands up and glared at both of their back. I can take a hint. They were pushing me away, wanting me to leave. Any progress my dad and I had made in our relationship this summer had been instantly discarded.

"Go stay with the Rogers while I get her settled." My dad tossed a look over his shoulder, but it only lasted a moment before he turned back to my mom, and they disappeared into the house. The door shut behind them. Neither of them looked back.

I planted my feet to the ground with my hands on my hips, and I glared at my house, hating everything about this place. Across the yard, Eddie ran out of his house and looked toward me while jerking a thumb over his shoulder. "Abs, go inside before she sees you again."

I was stuck. My feet didn't move. I was mad at my dad. Mad at my mom. Embarrassed the Rogers had to see that. But even more than being physically stuck standing in the dirt, I was stuck in this life

Chapter Twenty-Two

Linda set down a mug of hot cocoa topped with homemade goat's whipped cream in front of me. "Here you go."

I slumped down in my chair at the kitchen table with my back to their front door. I didn't want to even look at my house. I wasn't welcome there.

"Did you get a chance to eat anything for lunch?" Linda stood back with her focus still on me. "I can make you some oatmeal, or I have some leftover meatloaf and potatoes."

"I'm not hungry." I raised my cup and slowly blew on my hot cocoa. The whole goat milk thing was still completely disgusting to me, but I would never say a negative word to Linda. Not after all the ways she'd gone out of her way to help me. "But thank you."

"You're welcome." She turned to the tiny stove behind her and wiped her hands on the towel that hung over the handle.

"I don't know what Dad's going to do this time." I vented, my voice bitter. "Usually I go to school to get away from her. Then I hide in my room or go to a friend's house. I can't hide anywhere here."

Millie came down the little steps from her loft and padded over and plopped down on a chair next to me. "Maybe he can hide her."

I get that she's trying to help, and she thought it was a real solution, but the corners of my lips tugged up slightly because the thought of stashing my mom somewhere I wouldn't have to see her again seemed totally enticing. I sipped from my mug, trying to comprehend what had happened. "I can't believe I can't go home."

"You can stay here," Linda offered. "We have the sofa, or if you want to sleep in Fulton's recliner, we haven't moved it back in the house yet. He always said it was comfortable."

Her little smile was so warm and comforting, it should have made me feel better, but in a way, I felt worse. She was giving me a sample of what other mothers were like, reminding me of what I'd missed out on. "I'll try the recliner, if that's okay."

"It's all yours." She gestured toward the front porch before grabbing a bundle of fabric that had been folded on the counter. "I've been meaning to ask you for an opinion on the skirt I'm sewing for Mille." She unfolded the denim skirt, stretching it out on the table in front of me. "She wants something on her jean skirt to spice it up a bit."

"It's pretty thick fabric." I rubbed the edge of the fabric, feeling the weight. "You're the seamstress. Not me."

"I can sew, but I don't know what's in fashion like you do. Millie loves everything about your style. I want this to be special for her. What would you do?"

I shrugged. Man, it felt like elephants had been sitting on my shoulders all day, and I really didn't want to sew or talk about sewing, but Linda was being so nice to me, I gave her my honest opinion. "This fabric is coarse. I'm not sure you'd want to add anything to it, because it would bulk it up more." I grabbed the skirt by the waist and held it up to eye level, studying the stitching to see what had to stay and what could be removed. "What if we tried a cut-out on the pocket." I slid my finger into the pocket to see how deep it was, and added, "That would work."

"I like it." Linda nodded. "What are you thinking?"

"What if we did something modern like a thin zigzag and then sewed a patch behind it so it popped the color through it?"

"Love that idea." Linda reached into her sewing basket, pulling out her fabric cutter and a pencil. "Here, go ahead and mark what you're thinking about."

She was trying to distract me again. I didn't have anything else to do, so I set my hot chocolate out of the way and leaned over the fabric. I knew exactly how it should look and quickly sketched out a couple lines on each pocket. When I was done, I slid the skirt back to her. "Here, you can cut it; I don't think my hands are that steady."

I thumbed through her fabric scraps to find something to make a patch, and asked Millie, "Do want a pop of color like pink or red, or something neutral like white or gray?"

"I want pink." Milie leaned over the samples with me and pulled out a flamingo-colored fabric.

"I think that's all we need then. You can sew it right inside the pocket, and bam, it's an original design."

"An original Aubergine design," Linda said.

"You sound like my dad now." I spotted my mug, tucked behind the sewing basket and retrieved it. "I could help you with that. If you have an idea, tell me what you want me to do. It worked for us just now. Look how cool this is."

She held up the skirt and pulled at the pocket, revealing one of the zigzags with the patch placed behind it. "We make a good team."

Eddie came through the front door, carrying a bundle of clothes, and looked anxiously at me. "I managed to grab a few of your things for the night. Your dad said you liked this blanket to sleep with."

"Thank you." I took the pile of stuff into my lap. I wasn't expecting good news, not so soon anyway, but I had to ask, "How are things over there?"

"It's pretty rough." Eddie let out a breath like he had digested something sour. "She sees things so black and white, and there's no convincing her any other way.,

"That's what she does. It's best to let her be then."

"I don't know how you can. She's not okay." Eddie's eyes were frightful, and I didn't doubt he saw my real mom tonight. "There's no way we can go through this all night."

"It's better to call an ambulance." I looked first at Eddie and then at Linda, who slid her chair back, opened the fridge and proceeded to pull out glass containers of food. I think I have her figured out. Whenever things go wrong, she just feeds people. It's not a bad habit to have, and it beats screaming and yelling like my mom does. Eddie just stood in the doorway, shifting his weight from one foot to the other. Poor guy. He had no idea what he was getting into. "Look," I said, "Nothing is going to help. One of the therapists she saw in New York said it was the scorched-earth syndrome. It's like she hates you so much that she wants to get rid of you. She doesn't care if she has to burn everything down, destroying herself in the process." I flicked my fingers open like exploding fireworks and made a convincing explosive noise. "She must win."

Eddie nervously scratched his head like he had just learned I had lice.

"Here's some food." Linda placed the tray in Eddie's hands. "You need to stay over there tonight to give Cole support. I'll keep the girls here."

Eddie's eyes dropped to the tray covered in the different brightly colored containers of food. "I'm not trained for this. That woman needs professional help."

"Maybe you need to go back there to convince Cole to call help then," Linda said. "But don't leave him alone." Linda waited until the door had shut behind Eddie, and she turned to me. "Sorry if that was hard for you to hear. He doesn't always think before he speaks."

"Don't worry about me hearing it. I've lived it my whole life."

We stayed up late sewing. Every time we finished a project, Linda automatically remembered something else she wanted my opinion on. After the third round, I realized she didn't need my help at all, but she was trying to keep my mind occupied and my spirits lifted.

After midnight, I snuggled into Fulton's recliner with my hug blanket. Their front porch was actually cozy, with the screened windows. Thousands of silver stars twinkled down at me as if they too were trying to bring me happiness, but then there was the contrast of my house across the yard that seemed to have a voice of its own, taunting me, telling me how much my mom hated me.

I pressed the softness of my blanket to my face and closed my eyes, willing myself to let go of the day. It was weird, because the more I let go of my mom drama, the more I felt what was underneath that. I missed Fulton. Being here in his little chair only reminded me more of him, and my heart sank to a new low. Things on the farm were only getting worse every day. At what point does my dad just give up and say this was a mistake?

Tapping. I cracked my eyes open. It was my dad at the porch door. Still wearing the same shirt he had on last night; he was starting to look homeless. Well, maybe not homeless, but he never looked this unkept in New York. His face was shadowed with even more whiskers, and the circles under his eyes were so dark, his skin looked two-tone. I waved at him to come inside, and he opened the door, and spoke softly, "You should've locked this last night."

I shielded my eyes with my hand, screening the morning sun, and mumbled, "Sorry."

"Good news." He knelt next to the chair, but I wasn't convinced anything he had to say was good. I kept my face even, ready to be the judge of this news. "I found somewhere to take mom," he said. "There's a home, sort of like a group home, where we can take her. All the employees are specially trained, and they have better security than Evergreen. It's quiet there too. Lots of therapy for her."

Refusing to get my hopes up, I give him a side-eye. "You think that's going to be better than the hospital?"

"I do. She doesn't do well with high-level hospital care, but Evergreen was too lax. This seems like it might be a nice fit. It's super expensive though, but it'll be worth it if it helps. The bad news is that she can't get in until the first of the month—"

"That's a whole week," I cut him off. I almost chuckled out loud as I can't believe he's trying to sell this as good news. "So, what's the plan for me. Am I supposed to just live on this porch?"

"I wish I could have you come home, but I don't want to push her. So, I called Becky's mom and explained the situation. She agreed you could stay with them until we get Mom moved. How does that sound?"

My head jolted back, and I did a double take as I was *sure* I didn't hear that correctly. "In New York?"

Dad nodded. "I think you can handle it on your own, and it'll be better for you than being here."

"Are you serious?" I flung my arms around his neck to hug him. "Thank you! That's the first sane thing you've said to me in the last five months."

He held up his index finger. "On one condition."

I didn't even hesitate to hear his condition because I would do anything if it meant I could go back, even if it was only one week. I truly thought I'd never hear that offer come from him. "What do you need?"

"I need you to stay on top of your schooling. This isn't a vacation. Becky has school, so during the day you need to be online getting your assignments completed and turned in. If you don't keep up with that, you will not be allowed a privilege like this again."

"I promise." I tried to tone down my smile because I knew the situation with my mom was bad, but something good was finally happening for me. "So, when do I get to go?"

"I confirmed you a ticket on the last flight out tonight."

"Seriously!" I squealed, jumping up from my recliner. I couldn't believe this was really happening. I'm getting off this farm, and I get to see my friends.

"Shh! They might still be resting." My dad held a finger to his lips and motioned to the silent house. "It's the only flight I could get you on last minute. We can leave for the airport around dinner. Is that okay?"

"Yes!" I didn't even feel bad that I was excited to leave this place with my mom being sick. I knew no one needed me here, and I was starving for city life.

Chapter Twenty-Three

I landed at JFK airport early the next day. The thickness of New York air, so close to sea level, invigorated me. I got a huge, floppy thin-crust pizza from my favorite pizza stop. I folded it in half like a true New Yorker and ate it on the floor of Penn station, listening to a blues-inspired guitarist play for money. It had been ages since I was able to take such deep and cleansing breathes, and I sat there soaking it all in.

I was home.

Normally, I would have taken the subway up to Park Avenue to meet Becky, but it was morning, and she was at school. Since I had time to kill, I decided to walk. All my belongings fit into my backpack, so I didn't have to mess with luggage, and I practically skipped along the way. I got goosebumps as I ascended the escalator out of Penn station. Ever since I was a little girl, this had always been one of my favorite ways to enter the city. I watched the buildings stretch ever taller until I had to tip my head all the way back. That was what I called majestic. *I didn't miss my mountains at all.*

While I walked, I held my new phone and glanced at it periodically like the old days when it had been an extension of my hand. Dad had gifted me the phone for my trip. The best part was that he never said anything about me having to give it back when I got back to Montana. I hoped I would never have to be without it again.

After spending most of the day window shopping on my way to Becky's house, I only had to wait a short while at her house before I spotted her walking home from school. She saw me too and shouted, "Aubergine! You beautiful thing!"

I smiled so big I thought I'd break my face, and I ran toward her. "Becky! I can't believe how much I missed you." I wrapped my arms around her shoulders and squeezed hard.

"Welcome home." She pulled away from me and grabbed my hand, propelling me forward into their condo lobby. "I can't wait to tell you everything you've missed. I can't believe you don't even have social media. It's like you fell off the planet." We sped walked through the lobby and past the elevators, talking as fast as she walked, "It's way faster to take the stairs."

"I feel like I fell off the earth. I'm so glad to be back." We climbed the stairs as fast as we could to the third floor and then bee-lined to her condo. Once we got inside, the housekeeper greeted us, but Becky yanked my arm past the maid until I was in her bedroom. She shut her bedroom door and then squealed, "Abs! You're here. Tell me everything."

Out of breath, I just stood there, feeling as if I was in a dream. I looked around her bedroom. Except for a new laptop, nothing had changed. I dropped my bag on the floor and crossed the room, making myself at home just like I used to do, by flopping on her sunflower bedspread, and laying back.

She plopped down on her bed next to me, hugging her legs in front of her. "So, guess what new gossip I have from today?"

"I have no idea; I've missed the whole summer."

"You remember Madeline from our cheer squad?" She gestured forward as her eyes sparkled, teasing all the gossip.

"The one who was always a little too sharp with her arm movements?"

"That's her." She made a high V above her head and over-exaggerated a switch into a low V, making fun of her. "She was demoted this year to the base of the pyramid because she gained weight over the summer. But it turns out she's stable to stand on, and she didn't really complain about it once it happened anyway. Well, nobody paid any attention to her anymore because she was the bottom of the pyramid girl, and apparently, she lost a lot of weight in the last month and passed out at school this morning." She widened her eyes to illustrate how shocking this news was, then continued: "She got to ride in an ambulance to get checked out. They found out she hadn't eaten anything for like three weeks—well except for rice cakes and water—and so she was, like, on an IV at the hospital. Her mom called the school and got mad at Mrs. Kelly and said it was her fault for making her be the base girl. Can you believe that?" Becky rambled so fast I had a hard time keeping up with her.

"Is she going to be okay?"

"I don't know." She shrugged her shoulders, making her dangly earrings jingle. "I think it's crazy they blamed Mrs. Kelly. It's her own fault, don't you think?"

My head was still spinning, trying to follow the details of her story. I didn't remember Becky talking so fast before. I said, "It seems sort of mean to demote someone who was a decent flyer just because she gained some weight. I mean, how much weight are we talking about?"

Becky's eyes got even wider. "I'd say at least seven to ten pounds."

"That doesn't really seem like a big deal then."

She stared at me as if she was just meeting me for the first time. "I can't believe you don't think so."

I stretched out sideways on her bed and pulled a pillow under my arm. "I don't think it's that big of a deal. So, what else is new?" The bedroom door flung open, and Tina burst through the doorway.

"Abs, it's you!" she squealed.

I sprang to my feet and jumped in excitement. She grabbed me in a ginormous hug and squeezed so hard it made me hold my breath. "How are you, you gorgeous girl?"

I grinned with new enthusiasm. "I'm better now that I'm here."

"I freaked when I heard you were coming home. It's been so weird without you," Tina said.

"It's been weird not being here," I said.

Tina sat crossed leg on the floor. "So, what's it like living in the country?"

I followed her lead and relaxed back into the bed. "It sucks." I wanted to elaborate but something made me stop. It was because I knew Tina too well. I wanted to tell her all about how horrible it was having to scavenge for food, and not shop and not have internet, but I knew she would make fun of me. I didn't dare tell them about the composting toilet, drinking goat's milk, or what happened to my mom.

"What sucks about it?" Becky leaned toward me. The look on her face reminded me of a dog salivating over a piece of T-bone steak. She was dying for juicy details.

I couldn't think of anything safe to tell them about my new life, so I focused on my old life. "It sucks being away from you two," I said, truthfully. "I've missed you guys, I've missed school, I've missed dance. I've missed New York."

"I actually heard some rumor that Fulton is back and in college?" Tina raised an eyebrow toward me, waiting for confirmation.

I slowly nodded my head, feeling somewhat protective over Fulton's news. "Yeah, he ended up finding a way to skip his senior year."

"You should totally do that," Becky said.

"I thought about it when Fulton told me he was going to, but he had to pass his GED to get into college, and I don't think I can pass the math part of it. Plus, I'm not even close to being eighteen, so I wouldn't be allowed to leave home."

"He told you he was going to do that?" Tina wrinkled her nose like she had gotten a whiff of someone's gym feet.

"Yeah, he told me right away when we got there that his plan was to find a way to come back to New York as soon as he turned eighteen."

"It's so weird you talk to him." Tina's shoulders visually shuddered like she got the creeps. "Did you have to see him much?"

My face warmed from the tone of her voice. I knew she thought of him the way I used to—a huge geek who I would be embarrassed to be seen with—but now that I knew him, I felt bad Tina would speak so rudely about him. "I saw him all the time. We lived next door to each other." My voice sounded wimpier than I would have liked.

"That sucks for you. I'm sorry you had to endure that." Becky laid an empathic hand on my knee.

"You poor thing." Tina pulled out her phone and flipped through photos. "Do you want to see pictures of the guy I get to live by at my beach house?" She flashed her phone screen up to my face.

I recognized his face, but I couldn't think of his name. "Who is that?"

"Bentley Roads."

"You still like Bentley?" I was a little shocked, realizing yet another thing hadn't changed about Tina.

"His parents bought the house right next door to ours. We're always over there." Tina pulled her phone back and gazed lovingly at Bentley's picture.

"You should see the grounds on that house. He has the best pool. It's right in the sun with no trees, so it's always so warm," Becky added. "I love it there."

"It's awesome." Tina took one last look at Bentley before setting her phone down next to her. "And it gets better; my dad has been working from his west coast office all the time too, so Bimbo always takes us out there, but she likes her wine too much, so she ends up sleeping most of the day. Seriously best life ever. You're totally missing out."

"I know," I groaned. "My life stinks now. I can't wait to move back."

"You could totally live with Bimbo and me at the beach house. She wouldn't even notice if you were there all the time."

"My dad would never let me. I have to wait until I'm eighteen . . . if I can live that long." I dramatically dropped my face into her pillow. "I'm so jealous." I fake screamed into her pillow.

Becky and Tina both laughed at me. "Hey, so it's Friday. A bunch of people are going to the movies if we want to meet them," Becky said.

Tina looked at me. "What do you think? You get to pick since you're the guest. Do you want to hang out here with just us girls or do you want to go out?"

"I want to do it all. It's not fair I don't have more time," I whined.

"Let's make the most of the time we do have," Becky said.

"Deal. Let's go to the movies then." I got off the bed to grab my backpack. "I need to freshen up though. I have like no makeup on."

"Don't sit!" Tina jumped up from the floor and slid behind me. "You have something all over your butt. Like you sat in gum. What is that?"

"I do?" I turned, looking toward my rear, but I couldn't see any stains.

"I see it too," Becky confirmed. "Look in the bathroom mirror." She pointed to the bathroom door adjacent to her room.

I rushed to the mirror, turning for a rear view, but didn't see any stains. "Come here. Show me what you're looking at."

Becky walked in. "How can you miss that huge blob right there. It's all over." She circled her finger over the slipper patch I had sewn on.

"That's not a stain. It's a patch. I tore these jeans, and Linda helped me patch them. See? It's the shape of a ballet slipper." I pushed my hip backward to fill out the shape better.

Becky thoughtfully tilted her head to the side and studied the patch. "Why would you do that?"

"Do what?"

"Sew that thing on there. It looks gross. Why not just buy another pair?"

My shoulders carved inward in a cringe. I had forgotten what fashion slaves Tina and Becky were, but I understood their attitude because that's how I would have reacted before I was forced to give up my city-girl life. "Yeah, I forgot I had these on." I tried to sound casual. "These were jeans I threw on to travel in. I was going to change as soon as I got here," I lied.

I felt like an animal walking with my tail between my legs as I went back to the bedroom to grab my bag and pull out my other pair of jeans. I paused, embarrassed to unroll them in front of the girls because they were off-brand jeans from a big box store. I casually set the rolled jeans next to me and looked at Beck. "You know, I haven't been shopping in forever. I don't even know what the new styles are this season. Can I look in your closet for something to wear?"

"Sure." Becky eagerly whipped open her bi-fold closet doors to give me a tour of the hundreds of new items she had bought in the last several months. I almost drooled when I saw her closet was organized by color sections with everything neatly hung on matching white hangers. My hand gravitated toward the jeans section, and I thumbed through what had to be at least fifty pairs.

"Tina, come help me dress Abs," Becky said.

I wanted to hide my face in the closet. Becky was always the nicer one of my friends. Tina could be brutal when it came to her fashion perfectionism. I saw Tina's bewildered look aimed at my butt, as she tried to understand the shape. "It's a ballet slipper," Becky explained to Tina.

Tina wrinkled her nose. "Aren't those your three-hundred-dollar B. Nelly jeans?"

"Yeah, I tore them, but I loved them so much I didn't want to throw them out, so I tried to make them last with this patch." I turned my butt away from them so they couldn't look at it anymore, which complicated my ability to dig in Becky's closet.

"Why wouldn't you just get a new pair? They actually came out with new washes this fall that are way better than that one." Tina picked up her phone. "Here, I'll show you."

"I don't know why it's a big deal." I forced my voice to sound bored with this conversation.

"It's just weird. Why do you want to walk around with a big blob on your butt?" Tina said as she laughed, and Becky giggled.

"Sorry!" I snapped. I could feel my cheeks glow when I realized how silly my homemade patch must look to them. Back home, I had no one to judge my appearance, and I hadn't realized it until now but somewhere within the summer, I had let up on myself and stopped judging my appearance so harshly too. Now that I was feeling the pressure to look perfect, I immediately felt insecure and was instantly made aware of all my physical flaws. "We don't have the stores you have here in New York, so I couldn't buy a new pair, but I can't wait to shop while I'm here," I added.

"I can't believe you would let people see you with a blob on your butt," Tina said, obviously not willing to let it go.

I felt like I was on trial for some horrible crime I didn't do. I was not used to being the one in Tina's and Becky's hot seat, and I blurted out, "It's not that big of a deal what I wear. It doesn't define me. It doesn't make sense to be mean to me about it."

Becky and Tina stared at each other like they just witnessed a UFO go by. Finally, Tina broke the silence by muttering softly under her breath just loud enough for me to hear, "Woah, Abs. You need to chill out."

I swallowed hard. She was right about that, but I didn't feel like chilling out with them anymore. Then again, I didn't have a choice. I lowered my eyelashes as I felt a disconnect between me and the girls that hadn't been there before. "You're right. I agree. It's been a long day. I think I changed my mind. I don't feel like going out. Can we just hang here tonight? Maybe find a series online to binge on?"

Becky closed her bi-fold closet doors and grabbed her TV remote, clicking it onto the subscription movie channel. "Sure, what do you want to watch?"

"Anything with hot guys," Tina said from behind her smartphone screen. I zoned out as soon as they pushed play and found myself daydreaming about sneaking away to meet up with Fulton.

Chapter Twenty-Four

Tina reached her perfect arms above her head in a morning stretch, then instantly grabbed her cell phone to read a text. "Bimbo said we can go to the beach house today."

I had just opened my eyes from where I had fallen asleep snuggled in a sleeping bag on Becky's bedroom floor. "What time is it?"

"It's nine o'clock," Becky replied from where she was sitting on her bed.

"Already?" I sat up, rubbing my eyes. "I feel like I barely slept."

"Maybe it's the time change," Tina offered, sounding bored. She scooted to the end of Becky's bed and started smoothing her already smooth hair while she looked into the mirror on the back of Becky's closet doors.

"I asked the maid to bring bagels and coffee," Becky said. "She should be back in a bit."

I self-consciously ran my hands through my hair while looking around the room. It had been a long time since I cared about my hair the first minute I woke up, and I was sure it didn't look close to cute. "That sounds good."

"Did you want to go with us?" Tina looked at me, her blonde layers perfectly groomed now. She honestly looked like a princess Barbie who'd won the genetic gene pool for everything perfect.

I was still waking up and my thoughts were slow. I thought for a minute. Not a long minute because both of their gazes were locked on me. "Um, so you're going for sure?"

"Bentley already texted me, and they are at his place." Tina flashed her phone, displaying a picture of Bentley and a few other guys together on a ski boat.

I looked at Becky. "Are you going?"

"I'd like to go, but I want to see you too. It would be nice if we could all go . . ."

Part of me had wanted to sneak out for a few hours to visit Fulton, but I knew not to bring up his name to the girls. I'd have to make time for that after the weekend when they were back in school. "Let's go." I smiled to conceal how overwhelmed I was feeling.

Tina instantly started texting on her phone. Becky jumped up, heading to her closet. "Do you need something to wear?" She looked back at me.

I thought about the few things I had brought, and I was mortified. I had forgotten how much energy I used to put into buying clothes and looking good. Now that I didn't do that anymore, it seemed overwhelming to spend so much time on looking perfect. "Sure, do you have something in mind?"

She held up a floral baby doll dress. "This is really cute, and it can fit over your swimsuit or you can dress it up with heels and jewelry. I wore it for pictures, so I don't want to be seen in it again, but you're welcome to flaunt it."

"I'll try it." Taking the dress from her, I felt the fabric and could tell it was expensive. I missed expensive fabrics and the luxurious feel they had. "I like it." I slipped it on and ran my hands down the length of the skirt, feeling pretty for the first time in a long time.

"So, what are you doing with your hair these days?" Becky's eyes didn't even blink when she looked back at me.

"Is it obvious I need a haircut?"

"I didn't know what you were doing." Becky giggled. "I thought maybe you liked it all bushy like that."

"It gets crazy in the mornings." I ran my hands through it again, this time more forcefully because I was mad at my hair for making me feel inferior. "I haven't had the time for a haircut, but maybe now that I'm here I can go to my old salon."

"How about you wear a hat." She held up a black wide-brim hat. "It's my Audrey Hepburn look." She slipped it on her head and posed with a pouty duck lip face.

"You don't think it's too much?" I asked.

"Do you want an honest answer?" Becky took the hat off and handed it to me.

"My hair is that bad?" I instantly started smoothing it again as my cheeks flamed warm.

The maid tapped on the door with the tray of coffee and bagels. "If we take these bagels to go and leave now, we can catch the next train." Tina handed me a raisin bagel loaded with cream cheese.

"I'm good to go," I said.

"Me too." Becky slipped on a pair of magenta flip flops and grabbed her purse.

We left Becky's place and strolled down the street together like the old days. They started chatting about the new cheer uniforms they had gotten, and although I wanted to be part of it and feel good about being here, something inside me felt the emptiest I had been in a while. I was feeling like an outsider.

When we boarded the Saturday morning train, it was fairly empty. Tina stretched her feet out to fill the seat across from her and immediately started texting. Becky looked uncomfortable as we sat in silence. After a few moments, she asked, "So is there anything fun you want to talk about? "I shrugged. "I can't think of anything."

"Well, how's your dad doing? Does he like being there?"

For the first time ever since I'd known Becky and Tina, I wished I had the sort of friends I could open up to about what was going on in my life back home, but unfortunately, I knew it wasn't the things they cared hearing about, and I didn't want to risk getting emotional in front of them. "He's great," I lied.

"Well, good," Becky said, then we drifted into a long silence that took up the rest of the train ride.

"Bentley has the best bonfires," Tina said as we all crossed Tina's private beach to meet them.

"Do you hang out with those guys a lot?" I already knew the answer to my question, but I was tired of being left out of conversations.

"All the time. Tina's in love," Becky teased, then her eyes brightened, and she pointed across the bay. "Look what Tina's dad bought for the Bimbo."

I followed her finger to find a ginormous sailboat tendering offshore, and my jaw practically hit the floor. "Who's sailing it?"

"We have a captain for it," Tina explained. "Bimbo doesn't want to learn anything about the sailing part. She's going out with friends. If you want to meet up with her later, I'm sure she'd love to give you a ride too."

"That boat is seriously like five times the size of my house." As soon as the words were out of my mouth, I instantly regretted them.

Tina shot me a weird glance but didn't comment. "There they are." Tina waved her hand in the air.

Bentley jogged over, wrapped an arm around Tina's waist, and whispered something in her ear. She burst out laughing. Then Bentley looked over at Becky and me and said, "So, ladies, you're just in time for volleyball."

"Want to play?" Tina looked at me.

"I don't know," I said.

"Come on." Becky took my hand, dragging me to the net. "You're good at volleyball. I've seen you play before."

"It's not that. I like volleyball, but I just had surgery, and I want to take it easy for a while to make sure everything's healed."

Becky dropped my hand but kept walking toward the net. "Suit yourself. You can watch."

I wished there was a wall or something I could have leaned on. I was feeling over-exposed in a way I wasn't used to feeling. I had been ditched by my best friends, but I didn't want to let them see my disappointment. I decided to casually walk the shore pretending I was interested in a low-flying flock of seagulls. They took turns swooping down fast and then, before they hit the water, would swerve to come back up and rejoin the circle exactly where they had left it. It was like they had figured out a way to dance in flight, and I was mesmerized by their beauty.

One chubby seagull who was making the most noise slowly glided down as if he was too cool to dance like the other ones. I enjoyed watching him. Suddenly, he squawked loudly out of key. The birds broke their dance and formed a wide V, charging in flight directly toward me.

It happened so fast I didn't have time to think. They were shooing me away with their aggressive flight pattern and squawking. That too-cool seagull flew so low over my head the air breezed on my face when he flapped his wings. I held the brim of Becky's hat with one hand, trying to keep it securely on my head. With the other hand, I swatted at the bird and screamed, "Shoo, shoo! Get away!" I jogged back up the beach. The flock hovered above me, their squawks echoing in my ear as if they were mocking me and they knew I didn't belong on their beach. Then, as fast as the attack started, it was over, and they flew back out to sea.

"Abs!" Becky waved at me. "I was looking for you. I have someone I want you to meet."

Relieved to finally have someone to talk to, I walked briskly over to her. She hooked her hand in my arm, steering me directly into the group of guys. I recognized most of them from school. Many of them nodded at me or said, "Hey." She stopped by a new guy I'd never seen before. He was tall and muscular, with a deep tan and bleached hair. "This is Rex. He transferred to our school this year." He had one of those faces that could only be described as aerodynamic, sort of like a horse.

"Rex, this is my friend, the one I was telling you about." She motioned toward me.

I waved and forced a smile. "Hi."

"Hey, Abs." He grinned at me, flashing his teeth, which were so big and white I thought they looked like dentures. "What's up?"

"Ah, you know. Just chilling."

"Oh, I forgot I need to play more volleyball. You two can chat." Becky patted my shoulder before she scurried away. She peeked back at me with a naughty grin on her face just before she got back to the net.

Crap Becky, you suck, I thought to myself. I reluctantly turned back to Rex. "So, how are you?"

"Fantastic."

"You don't play volleyball?" I asked.

"I play football. That's why I transferred schools. I got recruited on a scholarship."

"You can get a scholarship for football in high school?"

"You do when you're good and the tuition's thirty grand a year."

"Oh, that's nice then. Where did you go to school before?"

"In Queens where I live." He nodded his head to the west.

"Cool." I scanned the beach, trying desperately to think of something else to talk about or a way to excuse myself. When I failed to come up with anything, I went for more small talk. "What else do you like to do?"

"I work out a lot. Today's supposed to be my cardiovascular day, so I swam laps for an hour."

"An hour? That's a long time." I forced an impressed look onto my face. "It wasn't too bad. I usually run for two hours, so it felt easy."

It reminded me how I used to dance for hours. I didn't feel like bringing up anything personal about myself, so I just stood there and smiled and said, "Wow, that sounds like a lot of work."

"Yeah, and then tomorrow's my leg day. I do legs two days a week and arms two days a week. Abs are every day."

My eyes must have glazed over as he continued to tell me in detail how many repetitions of different weight combos he did. I tried to look interested. The old Abs would have told him he was lame and walked away. It was hard to be new Abs. I imagined unicorns dancing around his head, leaving a rainbow trail so I could stay focused on his face.

". . . so that's why I quit eating dairy last year."

I caught the tail end of his sentence because the word dairy stuck out. I missed real dairy. "Fascinating," I said.

"Abs!" Tina called. "We're going to get some food. You want to come?"

"Yeah, I want to get out of here," I said, meaning it in more ways than one. I walked away from Rex without so much as a look back.

Chapter Twenty-Five

Monday couldn't come fast enough. As soon as Becky left for school, I scheduled a haircut at my favorite salon. Once that was done, I texted Fulton. He was excited to hear from me and invited me over.

As soon as I saw his friendly smirk, relief washed over me. "It's awesome you're here," he said when he opened the door. I let out a giant breath of relief. Sure, I was a tad froze in place as I stared at him. He had a new haircut and was wearing all college athleisure attire, something I'd never see him wear before. As much as his smile was the same, he had changed in other ways. He looked older and definitely cleaner cut than he had back on the farm.

He looked better.

Maybe even snuggly. I shuddered a little as my mind wasn't trained to think of him like that. He was my friend. My close friend. My friend I was so happy to see that I couldn't stop smiling as I walked inside his apartment-styles dorm. We stood in a micro kitchen. I could see from where I was standing there were two bedrooms directly adjoining the kitchen and a bathroom on the other side. "This place is nice." I eventually said, even though my gut was in knots because I was insanely jealous.

"I'm getting used to it. Compared to our tiny homes, this feels like a mansion." He leaned one shoulder against the fridge and crossed his arms over the front of his chest. "I can't believe you took time away from your busy New York schedule and life with your friends to visit me. I bet you're having a blast."

Swallowing, I tried to rid my throat of the dryness. Yesterday was anything but a "blast." It was hard to think about, but even harder to explain. I doubted that Fulton actually cared about my friends, so I just smiled and said, "Something like that." Then I quickly changed the subject. "How was your first week of school?"

"We didn't waste any time getting to the work part. I told myself that since it's a community college, it would be more like high school, but it'll be a challenge."

A guy with full facial hair and frizzy dark hair that buzzed out in all directions emerged from the far bedroom. Without acknowledging me, he walked past me, leaving the apartment. "That was Griz," Fulton said to me as soon as the door was closed. "He's not the most social person."

"I can't understand why you would give him that nickname," I said, sarcastically.

"It confuses me too." Fulton's smile softened into one that I recognized from the farm. It's the one he wore when it was just the two of us, and it instantly sent a whoosh to my gut. He tilted his head toward me a measure, and said, "So, what do you have on your city-girl agenda today?" Before I could answer, someone knocked on the door, opening it at the same time.

Two tall blonde girls, who looked like they could have been twins, appeared in the doorway. "Are you ready, Rod?" the girl with the blondest hair asked as she stood on one foot and stuck her head in the room in search for Rod.

I looked behind me, waiting for Rod to come out of one of the bedrooms. When no one appeared, I looked back at Fulton, who was giving me a strained smile.

"Is Rod missing?" I asked.

"No, sorry. It's just bad timing. They want me to go with them and some other friends to the movie at the student center. I told them yesterday I would."

Still confused, I fumbled for words. "I don't get it. Why did they call you Rod?"

"Rogers." He gestured forward as if I was missing a punch on the funniest joke ever. "They like it shortened."

"That's not really shortened. It's just sort of dumb," I said but then bit my lip when I realized I sounded rude. Then it hit me.

Fulton already had plans.

I was crashing them.

"But, hey, it's cool with me." I took a step toward the door while heat crept back into my cheeks. "If you have plans, I can catch up with you another time." I felt so naïve that I had assumed Fulton wanted to hang out with me now that he had his old life back. I flicked my hand up in a quick wave and walked right between the girls and out the door.

"Wait," Fulton called with an amused chuckle braided into his tone

"I'll text you later this week before I leave. Maybe we can have lunch or something." I tried to sound casual as I looked back, forcing myself to look excited. "It actually works perfectly because Tina wanted me to meet her at the football game tonight, so I have time to get there if I leave now." I waved again, turned on my heel, and walked toward the stairway door. I rushed through it and had the door almost all the way closed when Fulton caught up to me.

"Wait." He commanded as he pushed the door open. "Why are you leaving?"

Was he really going to make me explain this? Could he not see how awkward that was? I crashed his date, and I just want to disappear. I tried forcing my voice to sound normal, but it cracked when I said, "You have plans and I should meet Tina."

His gaze stayed locked on me as it bounced around my face, and he took another step closer, bringing the scent of soft amber musk with him. When did he start wearing cologne? I wasn't complaining about the smell, because it was amazing. For the second time in this exchange the word snuggly came to my mind, but I pushed it away. I don't need to think of him like that. He's my friend. My friend who has just changed so much, even in the short time since I've seen him, and everything feels weird.

"Something's bothering you." He reached out and touched my forearm as if that would have the action to keep me from fleeing. He was never a touchy person before. I stared at his hand on my arm, and my stomach dropped. I had wanted to come back to New York to see how it was, but everyone and everything was so different.

"Nothing." I tried to go down another step, but he moved quickly, blocking me. By now the walls seemed to wobble, and I planted my feet to regain my balance. I had never had this issue before. My stress was toppling over, and I was so overwhelmed. He pulled back on my arm. Not hard enough to hurt me, but enough to make me flick my gaze in his direction.

"I understand if you want to meet Tina, but I feel like you're trying to make an escape from me." His gaze continued to bounce around my face in a way that made me feel seen. It should have been comforting as he's always been my friend, but it was incredibly upsetting because all it did was remind me of the friendship I had lost when he left. "Are you mad at me?"

"I'm not mad." My voice was unusually high-pitched and like a child I looked over his shoulder.

"I know how that looked." He nodded in the direction of his dorm room. "They're friends from high school. I forgot I told them yesterday I would go with them. It was super bad timing for them to barge in like that. When you ran out, I told them I would go another time."

I turned my face down to avoid his gaze. It made perfect sense. Plus, he wasn't accountable to me. He's a grown man who can do what he wants.

"Seriously, what's wrong?" He moved over another step, this time squaring his body in perfect alignment with mine. "What did I do?"

"It's not you." My emotions climbed up my throat. I didn't want to talk, but I also would feel terrible if he continued to think I'm this upset at him because the truth is I'm not mad at him at all. I just miss him. I guess I didn't realize how much I missed him either until I saw him, and everything came flooding over me. "I didn't realize I was so stressed out."

"Are you stressed about your mom?" His tone was so gentle, presenting yet one more reminder of all the way I missed him.

He really was the only person who understood what I was going through. There's no way I could tell Tina or Becky about my life back home. If I had a choice, I wouldn't have told Fulton either, but he lived through it with me. All the years we grew up together, he was always there, witnessing it from the shadows. He's the one person I don't even have to try to explain it to. He just knows.

I let out a sigh that felt like I lowered a bit of my guard. "The problem is this entire week." I anxiously pulled at the end of my newly trimmed ponytail. "I was so excited to come visit Becky and Tina and be back in the city so I could be my old self, but I can't."

"You can't what?" The way his eye bounced around my face like I'm the most interesting thing he's ever seen almost broke me. He was so entuned. How did I miss this all those years? Even back on the farm, we were friends, but I didn't see how good of a friend he truly was.

"I don't know how to be their friend anymore," I eventually leaked out. "I listen to the way Tina and Becky talk. They're always judging everyone. I know exactly how they think because I used to think like them. I'm not like that anymore, and it bothers me to be around them." Fulton waited silently for me to continue. "I see them exchange these pitiful looks at each other when they notice something about me that isn't good enough for them. It infuriates me. Not because they are making me live through it but because I used to do that too."

"It's okay. People change. You've grown since leaving New York." He gave the most nonjudgement nod I had ever seen, and it did everything to tug at my heartstrings again. I missed him so much.

"That's just it. Now what?" I blubbered as my mind goes to war with my past. It saw so clearly how everyone had gone on without me. Not just Tina and Becky but even Fulton. "I don't fit in here but I'm not a country girl either. I'm like an orphan suspended between two worlds and I can't go back to either of them."

"I had the same feelings you did when I realized I couldn't go back to high school, but I knew I couldn't stay on the farm either. I felt lost. It took me a while, but I eventually figured it out. You will figure it out too."

"How?" The hopelessness that crept into my chest was so heavy, it was impossible for me to get a deep breath.

"I think you start by asking yourself what makes you happy and then you take steps to move in that direction."

"That doesn't work for me because I don't know anymore." My voice was weak, like I'd already given up.

"You're rushing it. Give it time and you'll see." He jerked his thumb over his shoulder. "Come on back inside."

I was back to feeling awkward. My face burned again when I met his gaze. "I feel like I'm crashing your plans."

"You're not. Come on." His hand slipped down my arm until it grabbed my wrist and tugged me forward. A sonic boom I'd never felt before rocketed up my arm, and it took all the energy I had to propel my feet forward. I couldn't take my eyes of his hand wrapped around my wrist. Again, this was Fulton, the same guy I grew to love as my friend on the farm, but yet he was different. I had a strong whoosh of air burst through my lungs when he tossed a gaze back at me. "Let's go order in a bunch of preservatives we can eat together."

I tried to hold back my smile, but his dig at our life on the farm sent me back to when we'd hang out and were friends. I missed that so much. I reluctantly followed him back inside his dorm room. A new guy was standing in front of the stove. "Sup." He nodded at us, causing one stray strand of his dark, wavy hair to fall in front of his eyes.

"You just wake up?" Fulton asked him.

"Yeah. I have night class."

"This's Wally," Fulton said as he jutted his index finger out toward the guy.

Wally glanced at me, then a look of recognition flashed across his face. "Is this the girl from home you were telling me about?" His smile dared me to laugh at his joke when he said, "Ab Machine?"

"What?" I asked, bewildered.

He ignored my question and kept talking. "Question for you"—he pointed at me— "because I know Fulton isn't going to know this great mystery. I got this contraption from the kitchen store. It said you use it to steam veggies." He twirled a stainless-steel veggie basket in his hands. "Now tell me, Ab Master Plus, how do I make it steam?"

"I'm pretty sure you should never give a girl a nickname with the word 'plus' in it," I said, unamused.

"You didn't like that." His smirk was unceasing. "How about *pro*? Ab Master Pro. That's totally you."

I grabbed the stainless-steel basket. "I better do this before your jokes get even worse."

He took an exaggerated step back. "It's all yours.

Fulton reached into the cupboard, grabbed a pot, and handed it to me.

I filled a pot with a little water and set the tray inside, then dumped in some veggies from the bag he had sitting next to the stove. "I would set it on medium-high for about twenty minutes. If you have carrots or other dense veggies, you can add another five to ten minutes."

Wally watched my pot begin to simmer and looked back at me. "I knew you'd know, Ab Machine."

I rolled my eyes at Fulton, who picked up on my annoyance and said, "I think the jokes are played out."

"Really?" Wally looked at me. "It's not funny anymore?"

I shook my head. "No, it never really was."

"But you're smiling." He pointed to my mouth with his finger so annoyingly close I could have bit it. "You weren't smiling when you came in. Now you are." When I didn't reply, he pivoted on his foot, reached into the cupboard, and grabbed a plate.

"I guess you're right. I am smiling now." Although it was true he had managed to distract me from why I was sad, he wasn't able to take away the awkwardness I felt about crashing Fulton's plans and seeing how quickly he had moved on from his life on the homestead. At the ranch, I was never concerned about if Fulton wanted to hang out with me—he pretty much had to since I was the only other person his age to hang out with—but here I wondered what he really thought about me, and if he still saw me as the mean girl.

Chapter Twenty-Six

On Tuesday, I waited until Becky went to school before I crawled out of my sleeping bag. A missed call from my dad flashed on my phone, and I pushed the call button on his number.

"Hey, how's it going?" he asked.

"Good." I relaxed on Becky's daybed since she was gone. I spent the morning by myself, and I must have needed the alone time because this was the best I have felt in a long time—months if I was being honest with myself.

"Are you sure..." There was hesitation in his voice. "Everyone getting along okay?"

I shot a look to the heavens as I had instant clarity. Fulton called you, didn't he?"

"Don't be mad at him," he started in a calm voice. "He was genuinely concerned about you. He said something about you not wanting to hang out with the girls."

"It's not that I don't want to hang out with them." I let out a sigh of exasperation. All I wanted for months was to come back here. Now that I was here, I was still unhappy, but he's not going to understand what I'm going through. "It's not the same as it used to be, but it's fine." Becky's window gave me a front-row view of Park Avenue. I paused and watched the city I loved breathe the rhythm of hustle and bustle that I had missed. It should have been exhilarating to be back, but I couldn't help but feel down. After a long beat of silence, I added, "I was having a hard day yesterday, but it cheered me up to spend time with Fulton and his roommate."

"Well, that's good. Do you have plans for today?"

"Not really." I blew out another breath as the thought of doing anything made me tired. Being here was exhausting. "I was going to chill while Becky is in school. Why?"

"I called one of my old clients. She has a woman's fashion line. I told her you were in town and might be looking for something to do. She invited you to tour her studio."

"Why would I want to do that?"

"I thought it would be neat for you to see her studio. Something to do."

"I don't need a babysitter."

"It's not. Trust me. She's busy. She doesn't want to babysit you. I thought maybe if you needed a break again from Becky, you could do that. Blame it on me."

"Becky's not even here."

"She's a super nice lady," he went on. "Her studio's right off Seventh Avenue."

I sighed so heavily it was more like a huff. "I guess I can go. Text me the info."

"I'll do that."

"How's Mom?" I'm not sure why I asked, and as soon as it was out, I held my breath.

"I think she's finally ready to admit she needs more treatment. I can move her in tomorrow."

"That's good news," I said with the least amount of emotion possible.

"I hope this time's different."

"It has to be unless you want to get me my own apartment here in the city," I was only halfway joking.

"I don't think that'll be necessary," my dad said. "But don't worry about that stuff. Enjoy the last two days you have in the city."

"I'll try."

"And get ahold of Gabby."

"Fine." I clicked the end button on my phone and dropped it in my lap. Within seconds, it beeped with my dad texting me that I had an appointment with Gabby in an hour. "I can't wait to be an adult to make my own decisions," I said to myself.

I borrowed another one of Becky's baby doll dresses. She had so many it was hard to pick one. I was out the door twenty minutes later and headed to Fashion Avenue. I found the black and gold sign to her studio and opened the door to a narrow staircase, leading above a retail space. I weaved through a shadowy hall to the back of the building that connected to an even darker hall with her business logo on it, and an arrow telling me to walk forward. I followed the doors until I found "Gabby Rue." Her door was a dark faded maroon and totally not what I had expected from a designer. I almost turned to leave when the door flew open and a petite woman who was barely five foot two with heels opened the door and waved me inside. "Abs, right?"

"Hi." I waved.

"I was just about to leave, but now that you're here, I'll show you around first. Does that sound okay?" When she spun on her heel to head back into the room, I could see that her blond hair was so long it almost covered her butt.

"Sure." I followed her inside as I was still unsure what I was doing here. I did what my dad had asked of me. I was hoping she knew what to do.

"So, this is my studio." The wood floors creaked when she walked over them with her wedge heels. "Don't be creeped out. I know it's a dungeon, but I fell in love with the location." She pulled a string to turn on a single light bulb that hung from an opened ceiling beam, revealing shelves lined with fabric bundles. "I'm sort of old school with the way I do things, so I keep a lot of fabric on hand. I find when I get stuck on something, it helps to work with my hands."

She crossed the room again to a corner by the door. "Let me show you my computer. I'm switching over to a new design program where I can do a lot more work on it." She turned on a large tablet that was hooked up to a computer screen on her desk. "This is cool because I can do all my drawing on here and watch it up there on the monitor. Then once I have my designs done, I send them to a lady who makes a sample for me."

"You don't sew them yourself?" I asked. I had the sinking suspicion that I had been sent her for more projects.

"I used to do that. But the busier I get, the less time I have. I'm literally a one-woman shop right now. I used to have a team, but retail tanked so badly these last few years, I lost seventy percent of my boutiques and store contracts, so I've been running on bones now. She leaned against the low edge of her desk, facing me. Her face was childlike, with full chubby cheeks, an upturned button nose, and stunning eyes, colored like the Montana sky. "Some closed, some returned my items because they didn't sell. This can be a boom-and-bust job. I feel like I'm starting from scratch again."

I drifted to her mannequins, all lined up in a row by the wall. They were styled to impress with items I recognized from my shopping days. I reached out to touch the end of a marigold-colored scarf draped around one of the mannequin's necks. It was a thick, chunky fabric with textured spots on it. I almost drooled when I lifted it and felt the dense weight. "This is gorgeous."

"That's one of the items that didn't sell. I have ten totes full of them," she said, woefully.

"Why would this not sell? It melts into your hand like butter but it's fuzzy."

"Like moldy butter?"

"No." I shook my head. "It's perfect." I pressed the fabric next to my face and closed my eyes. "It's like a cloud scarf."

She smiled, but I could see a worried layer underneath her happy expression. "You're right. It is perfect. But it won't sell because of the way I constructed it. I need to retail it for forty-nine dollars, and nobody wants to pay that much for a scarf."

"How come so much?" I reluctantly let go of the scarf, wrapping it back on the mannequin the way it was originally fashioned.

"I've had a hard lesson about price points."

"Can't you just lower the price?"

"I might have to clearance them out on my website to get some cash flow, but it's going to kill my spirit a little because it goes against what I want my brand to be."

"What's that?" I walked closer so I didn't miss any of what she said.

"I want my fashion brand to be more than a fashion brand. I mean, I love fashion; it's all I ever wanted to do. I think back to when I had just gotten done with school. I was a naïve twenty-two-year-old with a buck and a dream who thought I could create a movement, but I quickly learned why they call it a dream."

Her passion-infused, storytelling style had piqued my interest. "What was the dream?"

"It started when I got an amazing opportunity to travel overseas as a buyer for a department store. I saw the conditions of the warehouses and factories, and it was devastating. I saw people, skinny as skeletons, slaving for ten or twelve cents an hour for these manufacturers, just so companies could buy cheap shirts for a dollar or two."

"I've heard some of the factories overseas have interesting labor laws," I concurred.

"Not interesting. It's pure slave labor." She shook her head. "It seemed wrong for people to destroy their health for someone else to get a cheap pair of jeans. I quit my job after that. I couldn't be a buyer anymore."

I leaned forward, intrigued. "Then what did you do?"

"I wrote down my core values. I knew I never wanted to contribute to an industry like that. I decided to do it my way." She crossed her arms in front of her. "I was stubborn. I wanted to be a designer who made beautiful, high-quality clothes that bettered everyone's life. I wanted my clients to love my clothes, and I wanted to provide real jobs that paid real wages."

"That sounds admirable."

"In a fairyland." She rolled her eyes. "It got out of hand so fast. First, I bypassed the manufacturers and contracted my own seamstresses for higher pay. I was flooded with applicants since I paid so well; I got the best craftswomen I've ever seen. Their work is so superior to anything else out there that I mean it when I say my clothes are the best quality. But this industry doesn't thrive on quality alone. You have to find a balance, and I have that issue of price; I can't compete." She looked down at the floor. "I thought everyone would be excited about my cause, but it turns out most people are happy to engage you in hours of conversation about saving the world, but when it comes down to paying for it, they don't want to dig in their own wallets."

"So now what are you going to do?" I waited in suspense, fascinated by her story.

She motioned to her computer monitor. "Thankfully, my online business is doing well enough. I don't need as large of a mark-up online. That's what kept me afloat. I have a few fashion bloggers who love my stuff, and they share anything I send them. That's how I'm paying the bills, but I'm eating noodles for dinner five nights a week." She crossed her legs in front of her and looked down again. "It's been a lot of restructuring. I used to be heavy with staff and merchandise. Now I'm doing as much outsourcing as I can so I don't have salaries and can pay as I go."

"Sounds stressful."

"It can be. Fashion's extremely fast-paced. You can't be afraid of change." She walked over to a clothing rack and flipped through the items on it. "I'm looking forward, not behind. One of my goals now is to have two separate lines of clothing—one that is higher end and one that is more affordable. My passion is still about paying my seamstresses more. I'll have the higher-end line to do that, but most people can't afford that stuff, so I need the more affordable line to sell volume. Make sense?"

"I think so."

She pulled out a nautical-themed dress from the rack. "Here's one of the newest designs for my affordable line. I'm designing a year out now, so it's for next summer. What do you think?"

I touched the skirt. "I can tell you used nice fabric. I love the way it feels."

"I adore the way this fabric feels, too." She hung the dress back on the rack. Then she grabbed a stack of magazines from a shelf next to her desk. "Here are hard copies of some of the press I've had." She flipped through one of the magazines to a page she had marked, then handed it to me. A model was wearing a dress with red and white flowers on it. "See that gold piping on the bottom?" She pointed to the hemline.

"Yeah."

"That's my new signature feature reserved only for my custom orders on higher-end products. I call it my gold couture line."

"It definitely sticks out."

"I want people to see something I created and know as soon as they see it that's it's a 'Gabby Rue.' Your dad taught me about that sort of stuff."

"My dad's obsessed with branding."

"He knows his stuff."

"He did say he had a lot of designers as clients."

"He was a busy guy. I was shocked when he told me he was leaving. Crazy how things change."

"It's been a crazy year for us." I closed the magazine and placed it back on the shelf.

"So, that's my studio. It's not much to see. Most of my work is up here." She pointed to her head. "Anyway, I hate to bail on you, but I have a potential new client I'm meeting this afternoon, so I need an hour or so to get ready for that. Let me walk you down, and if you have any final questions, I can answer them as we walk."

"You're not bailing on me. I understand. I appreciate the tour. It was cool to see it." I inched toward the door, waiting for her to go first.

"You're welcome." She grabbed her stuffed shoulder bag that had been sitting on her desk and hung it over her shoulder. "Let's scoot." She deadbolted the door behind us. For a short gal, she took big fast steps, and I had to push myself to keep up with her. "I love being right in the fashion district," she said.

"I was thinking it would be nice to be close to everything."

"It's the best, and it's totally how I saw my career when I started out on this journey. I want to be right in the middle of everything. I love it when I need a break and I can walk outside my door and go shopping to see what everyone's buying, what's selling, what's not selling. It gets me out of my creative slumps."

"I can see that. I always loved the energy down here," I said.

"Exactly." She smiled sweetly at me.

"Well, Ms. Aubergine, do you have any last-minute questions?"

"I can't think of anything, but it was great to meet you."

She led the way down the stairwell. "Your dad has my info if you think of any questions or need anything else from me."

"I can't think of anything I would need, but thanks for the offer."

She pushed the door open to go outside, holding it for me. "Alright, take care."

I walked through the door and waved. "Thanks! You too." I turned to walk in the opposite direction she was going and almost ran into someone. "Whoops!" I said, looking up to see someone I recognized. "Wally?"

He grinned, showing me his perfect white and even teeth. "Ab Machine."

Chapter Twenty-Seven

"What are you doing here?" I did a double take, making sure it was him. He was dressed like he was going somewhere important, in dark jeans and an untucked white button-up shirt. His curly hair was sort of tame, mostly staying behind his ears, except for one unruly strand that bobbed around in front of his temple.

"I like to stroll around to window shop the fashion district instead of going to the gym." He playfully patted his middle, and then tacked on, "Then of course, I grab whatever street food is on the corner, and it's all balanced."

"No, really. This's creepy. Were you following me?" I looked down the bustling street, hoping to see Fulton by his side. No guy would ever be on this street unless he was being forced by a female. With no sign of Fulton, only one thing made sense. "Did my dad call Fulton or something?"

His smirk softened into one that wavered between certainty and uncertainty.

Holding up my crime-solving finger, I tried to prevent sounding bummed out, "So, my dad called Fulton, but he pawned me off on you."

"Fulton had a super important microbiology lab he couldn't skip." His smile finally caved all the way as he went on, "I didn't want to listen to his wallowing around about how bad he felt, so I offered to meet you."

I looked at my phone but didn't see any missed calls from my dad or Fulton. "Did Fulton say what my dad wanted?"

"He said you're lonely and depressed."

I let my mouth fall into a gasp. "I'm not lonely or depressed." I could feel my face getting red. "I'm sorry he made you come here." I looked down the street one more time, hoping Fulton would come out of the shadows.

"Nobody made me. I wanted to."

"Why?" I gave him a side-eye as this whole thing was feeling way too staged. I didn't need to be babysat.

"I'm hungry and wanted someone to eat lunch with me." He pointed to the spread of restaurants lining the street. "So, do you want to grab something to eat?"

I cringed, knowing full well this was a pity lunch.

When I didn't respond, he said, "It's a no-risk offer. Free food. You don't have to talk to me. You don't even have to sit by me if you don't want to."

I told myself that he wasn't a creepy stalker, but just a really annoying person. I also figured he wouldn't leave me alone as I was sure my dad had insisted that I needed a friend to hang out with. I figured the sooner we ate, the sooner he would leave. I reluctantly said, "Sure, I could eat."

"Let's walk back this way to find a place." He motioned with his head. "What kind of food are you hungry for?"

I surveyed the blocks as we strolled, inhaling samples of street cuisine. Everything I had once taken for granted, and even had temporarily forgotten, was still here. I almost cried happy tears when I saw a cart with my favorite gyros. My mouth watered at the thought of the cucumber sauce. "This might be lame, but I want a gyro. Have you ever had one?"

"Yeah, they're awesome. Let's do it." He got in line and ordered us both a gyro. While we waited, we watched the pigeons meander the sidewalk, waiting for food crumbs.

"I had forgotten how tame birds in the city are," I said, admiring how they trusted complete strangers to feed them. It's one of the things I didn't know I missed until I saw it again, and it sent a ping to my heart.

Wally grabbed our gyros and a stack of napkins. We sat down on the sidewalk, letting a nearby building serve as a backrest. "What did you learn at Gabby Rue's place today?" Wally asked, then bit into his gyro.

I unwrapped my gyro and carefully squished it back together, making sure the sauce was not going to overflow. "She gave me a tour. She was pretty busy and probably thought it was annoying she had to babysit me, but I'm sure my dad made it sound like I was going crazy." I took a bite of my gyro, letting the flavors saturate my mouth. It was game over. If I was heart sick for the city before, now that I had a taste of real food again, I knew without a doubt I would surely die if I had to go back to the farm. My mouth watered more, as I shoveled another bite in, and I relished every bite of it.

"So," Wally tapped my elbow with his like we were the best of buds. It made me put my arm down close to my side to avoid that happening again. There was an amused smile on his face when he asked, "So, you want to be a designer?"

I shook my head, but that did nothing to stop the pressure from flooding in. I hate that question. Maybe if my dad wasn't on my case all the time, I wouldn't feel so much tension, but I felt like I was under a microscope. "No, I don't think so. My whole life I wanted to be a dancer, but then I had surgery this last year, and my body needs me to stop. I don't see wha the big deal is. I don't know anymore what I want to do, but my dad's reaching, trying to push me into something. I guess he means well." I took another, more gigantic bite this time. It was even more delicious. I didn't care if he thought I looked like a pig. I'd never see him again after today anyway, and this wrap was the best thing to happen to me in several days.

"I think you should be a scientist."

"Why?" I almost snorted at his comment. "Anyone who knows me would know I'd be the worst scientist."

"Then I could say stuff like Aubergine with her time machine." He paused, waiting for me to laugh, but instead I stubbornly lowered my eyes to hide my tiny grin.

"You never let up with the jokes, do you?"

"People say I come on pretty strong."

"I agree." I noticed he had stopped eating his wrap, and he sat back, watching me wolf mine down. I didn't care what he thought of me, andI had no problem relaxing with no filter.

"But the thing is, people always leave smiling," he added. "Even after they complain."

"Is that why you are like this?" I unapologetically licked my finger and part of my palm where the sauce had dripped. I had no idea what this sauce was made of, but it was like a liquid, buttery, gold.

"Yeah, I love making people laugh."

"You should be a comedian then."

"I'm in a comedic theatre group now. After college, I plan to have more time for that."

"What are you studying?" I was back to my wrap now, and I repositioned some lamb that had gotten pulled out from my last bite. It made me think of Millie with her baby lambs and how cute they were. Suddenly, the meat in my mouth felt chewier, and I slowed down my chewing.

"Business, for now. My parents think I need to learn how to make money. Because apparently that's what adults do."

"Make money?" I echoed and then forced myself to swallow the last of my chewy meat. I felt a little gaggy. My mouth was dry. I looked up at the food cart, trying to spot a bottle of water. I coughed.

Wally patted my back. "You okay?"

"Yeah." I swallowed again, trying to muster up some salvia to coat my throat. "My throat got dry." I tapped on my chest, working the last few bits down.

He watched me for a moment like he wasn't sure if I was going to barf or cry. Then he started again, "You ever notice how once you become an adult, people always ask you how life's going, and if you're working on making money or growing a family, people think you're doing great, but if you're not pursuing either of those things, then you're a lost soul? Like if I just wanted to focus on making people laugh, well, that's not productive enough . . ." He trailed off, like he had something specific on his mind he was trying to avoid talking about.

"Maybe it depends on who you are talking to." I was still lingering on the thought of eating Millie's lambs, and my stomach was twisting. I wrapped up the rest of my gyro and tucked it in my bag, saving it for later. The old me would have chucked it into the trashcan and not thought anything of nine dollars, but fast food was an extreme privilege now. I didn't want to waste it.

"I don't think so. I think society generally has an idea of what moving forward is, and if you don't run in those circles, you can get left behind." He finally resumed eating his wrap.

I hadn't expected such a thought-provoking conversation, and I backtracked the conversation in my mind to try to understand his plea. "So, when you say you want to focus on making people laugh, what would you be doing differently from right now?"

He thought briefly before responding. "I think I would not be in school. School was never the dream."

"So, why are you there?"

"Cause that's what you do in life. Sometimes dreams aren't workable. At least from how my parents see it. I mean, life costs money. Know what I'm saying?"

"I do." I scratched my head when I realized I was getting a double-whammy dream speech today as I had heard almost the exact same speech from Gabby. Deflated dreams seemed to be a pattern in everyone's life.

"You do?"

"Yeah, I know what you mean when you talk about how dreams aren't workable. My dream was to dance forever. I honestly saw myself in a tutu when I hit eighty."

"Wait a second. I wanted to visualize that." He exaggeratedly stared off into space. "What color is it?"

"Gross." I nudged him.

"You're the one who said it."

I rolled my eyes, but then flicked my gaze back to him. "Wait, how did I look?"

Pushing his bottom lip out, he gave a satisfied nod. "You look good. I mean, for an eighty-year-old."

A real laugh bubbled out of my gut, and it felt so good to finally feel a positive emotion, it cracked a tiny smile to bend on my lips. "That was my dream."

"Aubergine, the dancing queen."

My lips curved into a sensitive smile. "I actually like that one."

"Finally. ABBA wins your heart." He smashed his wrapper into a ball, and checked around him for garbage, adding a napkin that had blown next to the building. "What about The Beatles? Yellow Submarine Aubergine."

I shook my head. "Getting worse."

"I honestly don't think I've ever had this much fun with a name before. I love your name."

"I don't mind it."

He jumped to his feet and said, "Come on, let's go somewhere."

I got up and followed him. "Where are we going?"

"It's a secret." He walked rapidly down the street, stopping only to throw his trash in the garbage.

Chapter Twenty-Eight

"Give me a hint." I struggled to keep up with him, tripping over my feet several times, but he just pulled on my wrist.

"Do your legs even work?" His smile was all teasing.

"What's the rush?" I tugged on my hand, taking it back, but he was too quick, and snatching it right back.

"It's more exciting when it's fast."

I stumbled on my feet to keep up, wondering why I was even trying. The old Abs would have been mortified to be seen with someone like him. I would have told him to leave, but I was trying to be nice. If I was being honest, in a weird way I found myself enjoying the spontaneity of the moment.

"Here's a riddle for you," he started as we bobbed in and out of oncoming pedestrian traffic. "What's blue and fuzzy, the shape of a banana, but tastes just like a taco?"

I mapped out the clues in my head. "A moldy banana with Mexican seasoning?"

The side of his lips curled up even deeper. "No, that's gross."

My brows bent down, as this was too much braining for me. "What foods are blue?"

"Just think about it. You'll get it."

"I don't want to guess."

"Are you any fun, Aubergine?"

"Why am I not any fun?"

"Just try and figure out the riddle."

"Why?"

"Because it's fun. Tell me when's the last time you had fun."

I paused to think about how sad I had been lately. Then I remembered something. "Two days ago, when I was hanging out with Fulton at your dorm, we had a lot of fun."

He quickly wagged a disapproving finger at me. "That doesn't count."

"Why not?" If we weren't running at top speeds, I would have perched a hand on my hip, but I was seriously pumping my legs to hard, I couldn't do anything that might slow me.

"Because I was there. You were using up my fun."

"You can't use up someone's fun."

"You did."

I tried to think about another time I had fun. I thought about all the times I hung out with Becky and Tina, but I never even had real fun with them. We were mean girls, not fun girls. Wally was right. That was my problem. I needed to become a fun girl. "Has anyone ever told you that you're crazy?" I asked.

"Every day." He grinned devilishly at me. "Guess," he urged.

"A blue food. I don't know. Like maybe a moldy blueberry that's smashed into a banana shape but . . ." My voice trailed off when

I realized it was an impossible food combination. "I don't know. Just tell me."

"A taco," he held his serious expression.

I felt my forehead wrinkle with confusion. "Is it moldy?"

"No, it's a regular taco." He looked at me with teasing eyes. "I lied about the blue, fuzzy, banana part."

"That's dumb."

"Maybe, but you're smiling." Then he nodded toward the building we were standing in front of. "Let's go inside."

"Where are we?" I looked up at the brick building. It was relatively unimpressive as it blended in with all the other buildings on this block.

He pulled the glass door open for me and jabbed his shoe to serve as a stop and motioned for me to walk inside. "It's a small theatre company where I do my comedy act."

"Oh right, you said you were in a theatre company." This felt like the longest detour ever, but I shuffled my feet forward. Inside the building, the walls were lined with headshots of actors, comedians, dancers, and entertainers of all sorts who had performed here. "I lived in New York most of my life, and I didn't know this was here." I was a little awe struck when I studied the black-and-white headshots, recognizing most of the faces. I had performed on most of the stages in the city over the years, and this place was never mentioned.

"The theatre doesn't open until tonight." He walked forward like he owned the place, and I scanned all around for someone who was going to stop us, but the place was empty.

"Are we going to see a show?" I hesitated to go any farther, because I doubted we could go in without a ticket.

"That's the secret." He flung open an unlocked auditorium door then paused at the top of the graduated seating and looked at me. "I am."

"You're what?"

"Going to see a show."

I scanned the room for performers. The place was empty, and most of the lights, except for a few spotlights near the front stage were off. I planted my feet to the ground, refusing to go another step. We didn't belong here. Someone was going to catch us, and I didn't want to get in trouble. I can't imagine what my dad would say to me if I got in trouble while I was here. "I think we need to go back."

"You said the dream was to dance. I'm giving you the stage." He nodded toward the stage in front of the empty theatre room.

My nerves fired on. Everything from the fear of dancing to the fear of getting caught breaking and entering. "You're insane, and you're going to get us both arrested."

"No, I'm allowed to come and go as I want to do sound checks. Nobody cares. I practically own this place." He jerked his head back to the stage. "Go on. It's your time to shine."

"I'm not supposed to dance." Now I could plant both of my hands on my hips, and I did so with sass. "I just had surgery."

"Said who?"

"My doctor."

"Do you have a doctor's note?"

"Why would I have a note?"

"Just for fun. Dance."

"No, it's embarrassing."

"I'll close my eyes."

"How's that showing you then?"

"I'll peek when you're not looking."

I laughed nervously, as I was starting to feel like he was never going to give up on this. "You're like the weirdest person I know."

"But you're laughing."

Something about Wally's tenacity both insanely irked and lifted my spirit. I looked at the cozy stage tucked into the front of the room. It was tiny compared to most of the stages I had danced on. I looked at him and pleaded, "Promise you won't make a joke out of it?"

"I promise," he said in an unexpectedly kind voice.

I walked up to the stage. In a weird way, I wanted to savor it because I knew these moments wouldn't be mine again. I used to be the proud principal ballerina on the stage at Radio City Music Hall. Now, I was a has-been mean girl who was on a pity outing, but I was okay with that because I was oddly happy.

I stood in center stage, looking out toward him. I placed my feet in first position, and I paused, satisfied at how effortlessly I was able to do that. It was incredibly cathartic to stand there. I waited for the movements to come, but I couldn't do it. It was too private. Too personal. And too final. I wasn't ready to share that moment with anyone or even to give it to myself. "You know," I started, "I can't do it. I think you getting me to stand on this stage is all you're going to get." Disappointed that it was all I would ever get, too, I walked downstage to sit on the edge.

He crossed the room, joining me at center stage. "How do you feel?"

"I'm just not ready," I said, looking away.

"Were you afraid it would hurt?"

"No, I'm not afraid of pain. Dance hurts even when you do it right. Maybe I was afraid it wouldn't feel the same." I looked up at his face, expecting to see the mischievous smile I had gotten used to, but it was gone. In its place was a genuine, pleased-to-be-here grin.

"So, I'll take a rain check then. When you're ready."

My eyes surveyed the stage. I expected to get a familiar craving to fill the space with movement, but I didn't. I didn't feel anything. Not even sorrow. "Deal." I looked back at him.

"Okay, so you're not going to dance"—he abruptly switched to singing— "*Are you ready to get out of here?*"

I had no idea why he was singing but I wasn't going to argue. I followed him out but made sure to steal one more look at the stage before we left the room. "Thank you."

"For what?" The skin between his eyebrows pulled together, causing his flawless skin to wrinkle.

"For trying so hard to cheer me up. I think it worked."

"I had fun doing it." His eyes caught mine, and for the first time all day, I didn't look away.

We said goodbye and went our separate directions. As I headed toward Becky's house, I passed an elderly woman sitting against a building. She had a piece of a torn flannel shirt wrapped around one of her legs in a homemade tourniquet. It made me think of when my ankles were in casts. I wondered if she had broken something and how awful that would be to have to make your own bandage.

Homelessness was something I didn't have to see in Montana like I did in New York. It's weird, though, because I never paid any attention to it when I lived here. Then, when I moved and didn't see it, I forgot about it—until now, and something about her struck me. She leaned against the building like she was trying to rest. She had to be in her eighties.

I had a flashback, remembering how annoyed I used to get when I was shopping, and homeless people would stand along this street. I always avoided looking at them. Now it's illegal to ask for money, but before it was, I'll never forget the first time I encountered a homeless woman who asked for help. I wasn't paying attention because I was panicked to get to Lord and Taylor's closing sale, and she came up from behind me and said I didn't have to give her money, but she had two kids at home, and she'd really appreciate it if I could go buy food for them. I lied to her and said I didn't have any money.

At the time, I had laughed to myself about how pathetic she was, but now when I thought about that day, my heart hurt. It would have been nothing for me to buy her kids some lunch or even food for a whole day.

I quickly pushed that woman and her starving kids out of my head, but I was left with the elderly woman in front of me. I reached into my bag and pulled out my gyro. I held it out, offering it to her. I knew a half-eaten gyro was basically nothing to give, but it was all I had. Her eyes beamed back at me. She was missing several teeth in the front, and I wondered if she would be able to chew it. But she must have wanted it because she said, "God bless you."

A weird chill trickled up my spine that I had never felt before. "You're welcome." I smiled back at her and walked away. I checked my phone to see I still had an hour before Becky would be home from school. I didn't have money to shop or go anywhere, so I decided to go to her place anyway and wait on the concrete bench outside her building. I rested in the shade of an oak tree and smiled at people as they walked by. For the first time in a long time, I was truly happy.

Chapter Twenty-Nine

I hung up Becky's dress just as she returned from taking a shower. I took an extra second to smooth out the skirt as I admired the fabric one last time. This dress wasn't anything special. If it had been my dress a year ago, I would have thrown it on a pile in the bottom of my closet, but among the many small things that happened to me over the summer, one of them was realizing that you don't always get all the things you want, and when you do, it is good to appreciate them while you have them.

Becky had a towel wrapped around her red hair and a mascara stain smeared under her eyes. She stood in front of her full-length mirror and began her nightly routine, which required multiple rounds of lotions and perfectly braiding her hair, so she'd have the right number of waves in the morning. She looked at me in the mirror. "It was fun having you here, Abs."

"I'm glad I came," I said, truthfully.

She parted her hair down the center and twisted in the mirror to get the right angle. "What time do you leave?"

"I need to be there by five, so I won't have time to say goodbye in the morning. But thanks for letting me stay here. Tell your mom I said thanks too."

"I will. You can come back anytime . . ." Her voice trailed off like she knew as soon as she said it that I would never be back. Our friendship had changed. She felt it as much as I did. I had grown so much when I left our high school that I had also left *high-school Abs* there. Becky still loved being high-school Becky and wasn't ready to be anyone else. *That was okay.* I didn't judge her, because I used to love being a high-school girl too.

I re-organized my backpack to get ready for my flight, taking my extra pair of rolled-up jeans and placing it on my laptop, which I never even used.

"You didn't pack much for being here a week," she commented from her view in the mirror.

I sighed as I looked inside my bag. It wasn't even half full, but I didn't miss having a big suitcase to lug all over the city. "It was sort of nice to not have stuff to worry about."

"You can leave your blob-stained pants here if you want. The maid can throw them out."

I waited for her lips to tighten into a smile to show me she was teasing—it would have hurt, but I would've been okay with it. However, she didn't smile. She was serious, and that hurt worse. She was clueless to what my life was like now, and the thing that bothered me the most was that she honestly didn't know she was mean.

I tried to swallow her comment, but then I thought about the first day on the farm when I picked chokecherries with Fulton, and he called me out of my mean-girl behavior. That was a turning point for me, forcing me through my rabbit hole. He had known it would sound cruel, but he also knew I needed to hear it to help me heal. I swallowed the tiny bit of excess saliva in my throat and said, "You know something?"

"What's that?" She tugged on a section of her hair, creating the perfect fishtail braid.

"I made that patch on those jeans, and I'm proud of it."

"Okay . . ." She gave me a worried expression.

"No, it's not okay," I said slowly. "At least I did something productive with my time. Yeah, it's not couture fashion, but I know where it came from. Most of your clothes came from a sweatshop, where some eight-year-old girl was forced to sew fifteen hours a day to make a dollar to feed her family. You think that's better? How can you be proud of that?" I waited for her to answer me.

She let her mouth fall open slightly, but she didn't say anything, so I continued. "You and Tina were mean to me because I didn't have nice clothes. I remembered when I lived here, people called us mean girls all the time. I thought they were jealous of us, but they weren't jealous. We were terrible." I paused to give her time to reply, but she remained mute. I'm sure she was already going over in her head what she was going to tell Tina about my freak-out. It would be some story about how poor Abs lost herself in Montana.

I went on: "I've tried hard to change, and I'm happier now. It doesn't bother me what you think about my pants because it doesn't matter what someone wears. It doesn't define me."

She blinked a few times but still didn't say anything.

"I had to get that off my chest," I said. Then I zipped up my bag, plopped down on my sleeping bag, and stretched out to sleep.

"Sorry if that hurts you. I'm hoping someday it'll help." I closed my eyes to sleep peacefully.

Chapter Thirty

"I got a call from your school." My dad sat across from me at the dinner table the day after I got home. We were eating soup from a can since neither one of us felt like cooking. It seemed the longer my mom was gone, the laxer my dad got about the rules on the farm, and food in a can was now a regular convenience we indulged in.

"Oh? What did they say?" I blew on my spoonful of chicken noodle soup.

"They haven't gotten any of your assignments. Are you having trouble getting online?"

"No." I slurped up my soup, waiting for the speech. I knew I couldn't avoid it forever. I looked at him over my spoon. "I didn't have time for it when I was gone. It was so crazy. Plus, I'm not much of a school person."

"You should be doing your school every day," his tone was still mostly calm, but the inflections in his eyes told me his blood pressure was rising.

"The only reason I ever went to school before was because I had to, and since I was there, it made it harder to not do the work. But now that I don't have to physically go anywhere, it's so easy to ignore."

"You have to do something," his tone was a tad terser. "You're getting behind. It's been three weeks already."

"I know you're going to think I'm making a big deal out of this, but I feel like when I left high school in New York, I left school altogether."

"I'm not sure I'm getting your metaphor."

"It's not a metaphor." I wiped my chin with my napkin. "Something happened here these last months. You said it yourself; my real education would be from homesteading. Look at what I've been through: Mom went crazy, again; I had surgery; I learned how to do stuff on the farm; I gave up my best friends; and I even got chased by a grizzly bear."

"The bear chase was a little extreme."

"Right? How can high school compete with that?" I set my wadded-up napkin in my empty bowl, and leaned all the way back in my chair so I could look directly into his eyes. He needed to see how serious I was about this.

"I know you hate it, but you have to do it. You need an education."

"Fulton didn't finish." I stubbornly crossed my arms over my chest and waited to see how he'd walk back from that one.

"That's what this is about?" He shook his head. "He was eighteen, and he had a plan."

"I'll be seventeen in less than a month," I gestured forward, as my voice turned to pleading. "I can get a plan."

"Honey, I mean this in the nicest of ways, but I don't think your grades are good enough to get into college without a diploma."

"I don't want to go to college." I got up from the table and placed my bowl in the sink. Anger was bubbling in my gut, and I had to move to keep it at bay. If I threw a fit over this, he'd just throw it back in my face about how immature I was. If I wanted to leave high school early like Fulton, I'd have to prove I was ready, just as Fulton proved to his parents. I took a deep breath and swallowed down my anger.

"Here's the deal: life's not all about what you want to do," my dad finally started the speech I knew he'd give me. "You can't quit school and just decide to live. You need a skill. Sixteen-year-old high school dropouts don't get far."

I had a flashback of Wally telling me life was about making money, and I couldn't hold back a small grin.

"What are you smiling about? It's not a happy thing to talk about being a drop out at sixteen." My dad had finished his soup. I reached over and grabbed his dish and placed it in the sink next to mine. "I'm not smiling about that. I'm smiling about something a friend said."

"I'm having a hard time trying to understand you right now." He pushed his chair back and angled his gaze back at me.

"Me too," I said a little too woefully.

Raising both of his brows, he held them in pause, and said, "Promise me you'll get started on school tonight?"

"I promise." I wasn't giving up when I plopped back down on my chair and rested my chin in my hand. I was only buying time until I had plan.

After a short silence, my dad picked up the conversation. "I was able to reschedule with that farmer to get the cow. It's this Thursday. Do you want to come with?"

"I'll probably pass. It doesn't really excite me as much as it used to."

"Are you sulking now?"

I lifted my chin up toward him. "No, I wasn't trying to. Just thinking."

"About what?"

"Sort of about adulthood and how I was excited to be able to make my own decisions, but recently I've seen how you can't do what you want because there's an expectation for you to be a certain way."

"Educated?"

"That and have a job."

"Or you can stay here and live off the land."

"We both know that's not going to happen." I shrank down in my chair. "Is that what happened to you? Did you get sick of the expectations?"

"Not really. It sounded nice to do something different. Don't get me wrong, I loved my job, but after a while it all started to be the same. Wake up. Work. Get a paycheck. Go home. I liked the idea of having a life where everything was integrated together."

"Hmm." I rubbed my chin.

"What are you thinking?"

"You said it was okay for Fulton to leave school because he had a plan."

"I said that."

"If I had a plan, would you support me?"

He took a deep breath and let it out gradually. "Well, if it made sense for your situation, then yes, I would support you."

An oversized grin washed across my face, but I remained quiet, trying to prove to my dad how mature I had gotten. After a quite minute, he tipped his head toward me, and asked, "Do you have such a plan?"

"Not yet, but I feel like it's coming."

Chapter Thirty-One

I settled into a routine of making sure my school assignments were completed and uploaded on time. It wasn't because I wanted to, but I knew I needed to prove I was ready for whatever was coming next for me. If I had admitted I found it easier to breathe with my mom being gone, I would have to also say the same breath was tight when I thought about Fulton. There was a hollowness to the homestead that wasn't there when Fulton had been here. Something had changed. I had feelings for Fulton that confused me. The more I thought about my muddled feelings, the more it didn't make sense.

Fall turned into early winter, and on the morning of my seventeenth birthday, I woke up to find the first snowfall of the year. I sat up in bed, wrapped in my hug blanket, and peered out my window. Snow dusted our mountain in a blanket of tiny diamonds. The evergreen trees that scattered the mountain were freshly frosted, creating a winter village of trees, untouched by footprints, looking like time would stand still for eternity.

Although I would have never admitted it to anyone, I was awestruck by the morning landscape.

From my loft, I could hear the coffee pot gurgle, snapping me out of my daze and calling me downstairs. I walked light-footedly down the stairs like I was afraid any noise would break the winter magic outside. My dad sat at the table with one hand on his favorite New York Yankees coffee mug. The other hand rubbed the stubble on his chin.

I was about to say something when I saw a neatly placed present in front of my chair. It was the size of a book, wrapped in gold shimmery paper adorned with silver hearts. A gold ribbon held it all together, and it was topped with a giant gold bow the same size as the box. His eyes twinkled when he saw me. "Happy birthday," he said.

"It's so pretty." I held it up to see how meticulous the wrapping had been. "I don't even want to open it."

"I wish I could throw you a huge party or take you on the biggest shopping spree, but I have a feeling those things won't make you as happy as this. I know I've gotten a lot of stuff wrong in your life, but I'm hoping I got this one right."

"That was quite the speech." I gave him an impressed nod, as I really was feeling special just looking at this gift. He was never a big gift giver. This was a huge step for him.

Joy seeped through his smile lines like I hadn't seen in a long time. "Thanks. I've been practicing since I got up this morning."

"I don't know why, but I'm nervous to open it now." I slid my finger under the tape and lifted it, careful not to rip the paper because it was too pretty. Something told me whatever was in my box was going to be a life-changing memory and I needed to savor this moment. It was a black box with a smooth glossy finish, and it had a gold heart on top with the words "Gabby Rue" in the heart. "You got me something from Gabby." I got excited and ripped the top of the box open to find gold tissue paper.

Inside the tissue paper was a fat envelope, sealed with a golden heart sticker with the same Gabby Rue emblem on it. I peeled back the heart sticker and pulled out the card inside. "It looks like an invitation." I flipped open the card and quickly read the handwritten note inside. Then I looked at my dad staring back at me, and if I'd known better, I would have thought his eyes glistened. "What is this?"

"What do you think it is?"

"It sounds like an internship offer to be Gabby's assistant."

He nodded while his eyes shined back at me.

"I don't get it." My heartbeat sped up a notch. "Why would she do this?"

"You asked me if I would support you if you had a solid plan. Do you remember?"

"Yeah," I squeaked out.

"I know you think I love watching you suffer out here in the hills, but I do want what's best for you. I didn't expect everything to blow up with your mom the way it did. I think this move was good for you, but not in the way I expected. It changed you."

"It did change me." I swallowed, still staring at Gabby's note. My heart was slamming against my rib cage so fast, I put my hand on my chest to steady it.

"I think education's changing. I also know you have an eye for fashion. I understand that you don't like school, so I've accepted that college might not be a good option for you. However, you will need a skill and training. I trust Gabby will be a good mentor for you."

I hiked a brow so high and glared at him. "You're really going to let me accept this and move back to New York?"

"I am. I found a woman's dorm that rents out rooms for girls your age. Most of them are actresses or dancers, but I'll pay the rent for you if you keep up with your online schooling. The dorm's right in Chelsie, so you'll be close to work. What do you think? Is this something you want to do, or did I totally get it wrong?"

"How did you get Gabby to offer me this?"

"It was a timing thing. I called her to thank her for helping you, and we started talking. Her business has suffered drastically because of the economy, but she's got a solid customer base and she's a hard worker. I was talking to her about her new product line coming out, and we were brainstorming some branding stuff. She mentioned she was using an overseas vendor for her marketing stuff to save money. Then I had my idea."

"What was that?" I continued to clench my card with both hands. The card was literally shaking from the trembling in my fingers.

"I do what I always do. I offer them something they can't refuse on my conditions. I offered to do her entire marketing kit for free. All her videos, social media, everything. I usually charge tens of thousands of dollars for this package. She knew she was getting a good deal."

"Why are you doing that?"

"I said I would do it on the condition she hired you for an internship. I thought maybe it would be something fun you could do to get an idea what you wanted after school. I knew she'd appreciate any free labor, and sure enough, she couldn't say yes fast enough. As soon as she said the words, I saw your path. It all clicked: your love for fashion, your eye for design, you wanting to be back in the city. Then I thought, why wait until after high school's over when you can take high school with you? I know you don't have the motivation to do school, so here's my sales pitch to you: if you can finish your junior year on time, I'll let you start your senior year there."

"Are you kidding?" This was beyond the best news ever. It was everything I never expected or even dared dream of. It was life changing in all the best ways.

"No. This is an incredible opportunity. If you don't like it, you can always do something different, but you'll have gained valuable work experience . . ." His voice trailed off. "You don't want to go, do you?"

"I do." I quickly nodded.

"Then why aren't you smiling?"

"It doesn't feel real. Especially after this last year when it seems like everything went the opposite of how I would have wanted it to." I leaned over and wrapped my arms around my dad's neck. "Thanks, Dad. This is the best gift I could have ever received."

"You're welcome." He hugged me back, and if I didn't know my dad well enough, I'd thought I'd felt him tremble a little. I decided the jitters I felt were mine. My mind drifted forward to how it would be with me leaving for the city. I wondered about my job and if I could handle it. I thought about school and quickly got overwhelmed and pushed that thought away. Then I was left with another emotion . . . a curiosity to see Fulton. I was curious to see if maybe he was curious too.

Thank you for reading Dancing on Broken Ankles. Would you like to read what happens next? Follow Abs in her next journey in: "The Stars We See."

Also by J.P. Sterling

<u>Christmas Shenanigans (All Standalones)</u>

Mingle All the Way

Tis the Season to Get Married

Let's Not and Sleigh We Did

<u>The Coffee Loft Series (All Standalones)</u>

Pardon My French Press

No More Mr. Chia Guy

Truly, Madly, Steeply Brew

<u>Sweet Hockey RomCom (All Standalones)</u>

The Pucker-Up Pact

Shot Through the Heart

Come and Get Your Glove (Coming 2025)

<u>A Modern Fairy Tale Series (All Standalones)</u>

Royally Rugged

<u>Bosses and Billionaires Series (All Standalones)</u>

Maid for my Billionaire Boss

Upcycling My Rig-Pig Boss

Kissed by My Billionaire Boss

Marooned with My Celebrity Boss

A Heart that Dances Series (A New Adult Series)

Dancing on Broken Ankles

The Stars We See

A Heart that Dances

A Heart that Loves

Water and Stone Duet (A coming-of-age Series)

Ruby in the Water

Lily in the Stone

About J.P. Sterling

J.P. Sterling grew up watching old reruns of Lucille Ball and Mary Tyler Moore and fell in love with wholesome entertainment and slapstick comedy. She loves leaning into the over-the-top humor and full circle moments, especially if it means the underdog gets to shine.

Aside from writing, she's also a wife and homeschooling mom, a holistic dietitian, a former college professor and lover of all-things dark chocolate.

*No swears. Just kisses. No Blasphemies. *

Let's get social!

Hey you amazing reader! You are invited to join my private reader group for all-things clean books and friends.

Enter the group here:

https://www.facebook.com/groups/1500850764081965

Other places to follow me:

Instagram:

https://www.instagram.com/stories/authorjpsterling/

Facebook: https://www.facebook.com/jpsterlingauthor/

Amazon:

https://www.amazon.com/stores/author/B01N9TJXJN/about

www.ingramcontent.com/pod-product-compliance
Lightning Source LLC
Chambersburg PA
CBHW021650110726
47902CB00007B/1904